CW01652194

The Stables
Stewart Park
The Grove
Marton
Middlesbrough
TS7 8AR

www.mudfog.co.uk

Cover design by J.Cianciaruso
Printed by H. F. Stokeld Tel.: 01642.246127

ISBN 1-899503-68-4

Mudfog Press is a member of
The Independent Northern Publishers
www.northernpublishers.co.uk

Mudfog gratefully acknowledges
the support of
Arts Council England and
Middlesbrough Council.

ARTS COUNCIL ENGLAND
LOTTERY FUNDED

Middlesbrough
moving forward

Introduction

Dear Bob 2 is the sequel that had to be written once it became clear that the original **Dear Bob** (Mudfog 2002) was such a success that it was going to sell out. As it did.

Bert Ward, the author, lived at 7 Sunnyside Avenue, Grove Hill and he was 11 in 1932. His characters are fictional, but the street and town and world they live in are authentic enough. Bert's careful historical research and his reading of editions of the Gazette from that year have made sure of that.

As Andy Croft wrote in the introduction to that first volume: 'In many ways **Dear Bob** is a political novel. But it is also a kind of wonderful working-class situation-comedy.'

Teessiders, present and past, have agreed. Its author has received letters of thanks and praise from many Teesside exiles in different parts of the world. **Dear Bob 2** can only increase his mailbag. Mudfog Press is delighted to publish this second volume of May Gill's letters to her son in the Navy with their wit, warmth and wisdom.

Dear Bob 2

Letters from Home

1932

May Gill

Bob Gill
HMS Norfolk

7 Sunnyside Ave
Grove Hill
Middlesbrough

Friday 8 January 1932

Dear Bob,

Here we are again, the first letter of the New Year. How are things in sunny Devenport? It is cold and windy up here. Here's a nice topic for this weather. Did you know that the ice cream cornet was invented by a man in America who got the idea when he saw girls putting ice cream into holes in cakes. I've told your dad to keep his eyes open and he might get an idea to make us a fortune. Anyway he's just died. The American, not your dad. Ta Ta Pet came in with this riveting piece of information.

You will notice one big change on your next leave. Buses are taking the place of trams. Ta Ta Pet, who is a mine of information, said there have been trams in Middlesbrough for thirty years. Anyway the last tram between Stockton and North Ormesby went to the Parliament Road sheds with the Mayor and Mayoress on it and thousands of people lining the streets. We are told that they are now a part of Middlesbrough's history. So Sadie Quinn and me are kicking ourselves for not going and being part of Middlesbrough's history. I can see the history books now. A photo of Mrs May Gill and Mrs Sadie Quinn on the last tram to the tram sheds. The Mayor and Mayoress were also there. They are being sold for scrap for fifteen pounds each. The trams, not the Mayor and Mayoress. You'd have thought they were worth more than that. The trams I mean. Dear me, this is getting complicated. Anyway we now have more double decker buses and less trams.

And how about this? We have ten talkie picture houses in Middlesbrough as well as the Empire. That's another bit of information from Ta Ta Pet. He's a walking encyclopedia. I know I've spelt that right because I took a look in your dad's dictionary while he was out. He's still guarding it like it was England's gold reserves.

When they open the Sydney Bridge in Australia, and don't forget it was built in Middlesbrough, they are going to break a bottle of champagne over it out of the King's cellar. We lived in a house with a cellar once but we only kept coal in it. At least that's what your Granddad said and he spent a lot of time down there so he should know. Anyway, what's a bridge going to do with a bottle of champagne? There's lots of the men here who built it whose tongues are hanging out, though they are used to beer so I don't think they would appreciate it. It takes a delicate tongue like mine to appreciate champagne. Sez me. I wonder if it comes up to Mrs Turnbull's rhubarb wine. Break a bottle of that on the bridge and you'd know there'd been something broken on it. But perhaps not. People have to cross it.

Talking about rhubarb, the coalman's horse did a load right outside our gate and guess who got there first from the other end of the avenue? Mrs Smithers with her bucket and shovel and her acid drops. She really gloats. It must be telepathy. I was telling Sadie Quinn about it and she said Mrs Smithers reads teacups. I asked her what's a horse got to do with teacups. Nothing, she said, it's just a thought.

Well Bob, I must be going. Sadie's just walked in and asked me for a lend of some money. So naturally, being made of it, I asked her how much. She said a few thousands would do so I said I was a bit short at the present but what did she want it for. She said she's read this is a good time to buy shares in Portland Cement and Bovril. Well, you know, Paddy is a navvy so I thought she was pulling my leg, but she showed me the paper. So I think I'll buy a few myself. I'll look in Jimmy's money box. He's a little hoarder.

I'll have to go. I see the Duke of Gloucester is on leave from the army and he's going to spend a few weeks at the hunting box he's taken for the season. I don't know whether this is good news or bad news for the army. And with all the trouble we are having in India. Mr Gandhi has just been put in prison again. I don't understand how an educated man like him can walk around in a loin cloth. He asks people not to engage in violence to get home rule for India, which I think is a good thing, I mean not using violence, but Mrs Levinson calls him a dangerous agitator. A lot of leaders of the Congress Party have been put in prison as well. There's a lot of trouble brewing there. Stan Cole says we should leave and let them get on with Home Rule. There's more trouble in the world when you read about China and Japan and I worry that it is coming our way. Now I really will have to go. Your dad will be in from work for his dinner soon, and the jam and bread kid is waiting to strike. Oh, before I forget. Good news. The Reverend Lester has been appointed to the Avenue Wesleyan Church in the Avenue, the one we go to. So why is this good news? The Gazette says that wherever he has been stationed the local football team has had good luck in the cup. The Boro are playing Portsmouth so we'll see if he brings the Boro some luck. That's all for this time so tara for now. Everybody asks to be remembered.

Your everloving

Mam

PS Your dad said if I was writing while he was at work that he wasn't bothered about having his usual PS. So I am not going to tell you that Chelsea beat the Boro 4-0

Tuesday 12 January 1932

Dear Bob,

You will be at sea as I write this but hopefully it will not be too long before it reaches you basking in the sun in the West Indies while we shiver. I've been reading that in Germany Herr Hitler has said his party has 800,000 members and 15 million supporters and they are going to fight Bolshevism. Stan Cole said that Hitler is a fascist who wants war with Russia but there's no need to worry because the German Communists and Socialists are stronger than Hitler. Mrs Levinson, the lady I work for, is opposed to the Communists and Socialists but says there's no need to worry because the German President and Conservatives will keep Hitler under control. It's strange the way Mrs Levinson and Stan Cole see everything so clearly and can agree with each other and yet disagree with each other at the same time. After Ta Ta Pet puts in his two pennorth I know that I'll never understand politics.

Sometimes when Stan Cole comes in for your dad to go to the Cleveland I tell him something I've read in the papers and he flattens me by saying that you can't believe everything you read in the papers. Then he tells you something and you ask how he knows and he'll tell you the name of the paper he read it in. He goes to the library reading room every day and reads all the papers and he buys a communist paper. I think what it boils down to is that if Stan agrees with what the paper says then it is true. My trouble is that when I read the paper I don't know whether Stan agrees with it, so I can't tell if it is true or not. A lot of what Stan says rubs off on your dad, so being married to your dad is like being married to the truth without really knowing what it is. When it comes to politics, and sometimes it seems it is all politics round here, I feel like I am always at a crossroads. There's Mrs Levinson pointing in one direction, Stan Cole the opposite direction, your granddad who votes Liberal in another, and then there's your dad. Your dad is different to the other three. They tell me how I should vote, but your dad says I can make up my own mind so long as I vote Labour.

Well, that's enough about me. There's something happened in Redcar that I never knew about. During the war a Redcar airman Lieutenant Ridley was flying an aeroplane when he had to force land in the Libyan desert. Because there was not enough water for him and his mechanic he shot himself so that the mechanic would not die of thirst. A tablet commemorating him is being placed on the house in Coatham Rd where he was born and was brought up. The house will be called Ridley House. His parents must be very proud of him and sad at the same time.

I told you last time we have buses now instead of trams. It looks like they are going to be a mixed blessing. A boy has been knocked down and killed by a bus on North Ormesby Road. He ran out on the road. He was only twelve, poor lad. The same name as us, Charles Gill, but he's not related. He is the first to be killed by a bus. When you hear news like that it seems heartless to talk about something else but life goes on.

Things are serious in Germany. I didn't know that a country could go bankrupt but that is what the German Government is saying. Germany was made to pay reparations to the countries that beat them in the war but now they say their economy is on the verge of collapse and they can't pay anymore. So what is going to happen I don't know. Neither does your dad and that means the men who go in Stan Cole's shed don't know either. So we are just going to have to wait and see.

The Liberal MP here, Kingsley Griffiths, has made a speech to the Middlesbrough Brotherhood, whoever they are, about the need for moral courage. But what does it mean? There's an Army reservist has a letter in the Gazette and he is going wild. The Means Test Committee have taken 3 shillings and three pence a week off his dole and that reduces his reservist pay to two pence ha'penny a day for being on the Army reserve. He says he wishes he had never seen khaki. The same will happen to your dad if he comes out of work again.

Yesterday we were talking about the pictures and I was trying to make my mind up what picture I wanted to go and see. I did want to go to the Elite to see The Smiling Lieutenant with Maurice Chevalier and Claudette Colbert but your dad spoilt it for me with one of his wisecracks. He said he could understand why Maurice Chevalier was smiling, playing with

Claudette Colbert. He'd be smiling himself if he was in Maurice Chevalier's place. I suppose I would, the money Maurice Chevalier gets. But the thought of sitting there in the Elite with your dad next to me smiling all over his face put me off. So we are going to the Palladium to see Viennese Nights. We'll see what he makes of that.

The Gazette is always carrying adverts "What's on the Wireless". I keep asking your dad to get one but he says we haven't the money to pay cash and we are not going to get one on the never never. Out of debt, out of danger. That's his motto. I feel like telling him to stop going in the Cleveland and we could save up but that would be like telling horses to stop eating grass.

Well Bob, there's lots more to write about but I'd better call it a day. Ta Ta Pet, Sadie, and everybody else ask to be remembered. Not forgetting the jam and bread kid. I don't know where he puts it.

That's all. Write soon

Your everloving

Mam.

PS Portsmouth 1 Boro 1. This is the cup tie so there will be a replay.

Sunday 17 January 1932

Dear Bob,

You will either be at sea as I write this or in the West Indies enjoying the sun. It is cold and windy here. Just the weather for sitting round the fire.

I thought that to help fill up my letters I would start a "things I don't know" column like they do in the papers. Then I realised that I can't write a "things I don't know column" because I don't know what it is that I don't know. How can I write about things I don't know if I don't know what it is that I don't know? Are you with me?

Last Saturday night Stan Cole and some of the fellas that go in his shed to discuss politics came in for your dad on their way to the Cleveland. Sadie Quinn and me were going to the market down Sussex Street. Before they left they were discussing the songs they were going to sing and someone started them off on the Roses of Picardy. It has lovely words and a lovely melody. They sang it in the trenches. It's very romantic but very sad. Roses are dying in Picardy, But there's one rose that dies not in Picardy, It's the rose that I keep in my heart. I wonder if it is really about roses dying or about the men who were being killed remembering the rose that they keep in their hearts. It's nice to think they had a rose in their hearts to remind them of home. I'd better shut up before I get all weepy.

Anyway, it was them singing that, that started me off thinking. I didn't know the words of Roses of Picardy but I did know there was a song called Roses of Picardy. So if I hadn't known there was a song called Roses of Picardy I could have put that in my "things I don't know" column, except that because I did know there was a song called Roses of Picardy I couldn't have put it in that column. That's when I twigged. Are you still with me? So now I can write a column called "things I didn't know" because now I know that I didn't know. At least I think that's how it works out.

Things I didn't know. White boxers are not allowed to fight black boxers but the Albert Hall might allow Larry Gains to fight a German. I'll tell you what happens. The men here talk a lot about boxing or I wouldn't know about it. And of course Ta Ta Pet keeps me up with all that's going on.

A judge in a breach of promise case has said that offer of marriage and acceptance is like a commercial contract and alimony should be based on that. I asked your dad what a commercial contract meant. He knows these things through going in Stan Cole's shed. So he said it was like somebody offering to sell a bag of coal and somebody agreeing to buy it. That was a commercial contract. I said was you marrying me like you buying a bag of coal? I thought he would say no, but he said yes. So I said well if you had stood me up how much would the judge have said I was worth, and your dad said a bag of coal. So I said is that what you think I am worth and he said no, that's what the judge would have said and he's an educated man so he must know.

That really riled me so I told your dad a few things about himself that he didn't know before because I'd just made them up. He just grinned and then he said that the judge might throw in the price of a few sticks just to get me going. Well it got me going alright and I told him a few more things I just thought of. Then he had the cheek to ask me to darn a hole in his sock before he went to the Cleveland. Lucky for me it was in the toe not the heel. If it had been in the heel I would have had to darn it because I couldn't let him go out like that and have people talking about me. But it was in the toe where he could feel it but people couldn't see it. Anyway when he came in he apologised about the coal and said he was sorry, so I said what about the sticks. And he said he was sorry about that as well. So I said well I take back everything I said about you but I'm putting it in the bank for the next time. And he said what about my sock so I said give me it.

Talking about what wives are worth I've just read that women teachers who get married are dismissed from their jobs. Not men mind you, just women. You can guess who made that rule. And yet women can be MPs. We had Ellen Wilkinson until the last election. I know she's not married but I bet she wouldn't be sacked if she got married. Anyway she lost here and Jarrow Labour Party has asked her to stand there. Perhaps she will stick up for women teachers who get married.

I'd better shut up, this letter is getting too long already. Look after yourself. We are all thinking of you in sunny Bermuda or wherever it is. Ta Ta Pet and everybody else sends their regards.

Your everloving
Mam

PS Two football results from your dad. Portsmouth knocked the Boro out of the cup. In the first game they drew 1-1 but in the second Portsmouth won at Portsmouth 3-0. It looks like the Reverend Lester's luck ran out when he came to Middlesbrough.

Friday 22 January 1932

Dear Bob,

Here I am again with me acid drops as they say. I wonder if they have that saying anywhere else. It's funny how you get these local sayings like howee means come here. I think that is how it would be spelt. Then there's spondoolicks for money although Sadie Quinn says that is Irish. We've been having a laugh at the adverts. The one for Kensitas cigarettes says that if you smoke their cigarettes the ultra violet rays will protect your throat. It doesn't say what from but we've been cracking on that you will glow in the dark and so motor cars will see you and not knock you down. By we I mean Sadie and me. Anyway they have a crafty scheme to get people smoking their cigarettes. They are running a competition. Send in twenty words saying how good Kensitas cigarettes are and the best will win a motor car. The catch is that you have to send in the front of twenty of their cigarette packets with one word on each.

There's a lot of trouble here about the means test. Thousands of young men and women are leaving home because if they stay and their parents have money the sons and daughters are refused benefit. So they move out and they get the dole again. It's really breaking up family life so I am glad that you are in the Navy. If you were at home and out of work your dole would be stopped because your dad is working. When the ship he is working on is launched that will be him back on the dole. The communists and socialists are campaigning against the means test but I don't think it will do any good. It says in the paper that the councillors on the North Riding Public Assistance Committee get £3 a week and two shillings for every paper they sign, whatever that means, but it could mean every poor soul they interview. I think they should be made to live on the means test and see how they like it. There's a letter in the Gazette from somebody who signs himself Underfed Patriotism who says that he has one shilling and nine pence a week deducted from his army reservist's pay and two shillings and sixpence off his dole leaving him with one pound four shillings and nine pence for himself, his wife and two children. He's very bitter. He says they ask us to be patriotic but why aren't the landlords patriotic. At the same time there's a Savings Committee in Middlesbrough saying they issued nearly 82,000 savings certificates last year although that is down by 5,000. So somebody must have money.

There's another letter signed One of Them calling the working class selfish. He says the workers are having umpteen children so preventing the more intelligent classes who desire to improve the standard of living from having any at all. When I got mad reading this your dad said take no notice, he signed himself one of them. So I said one of who and your dad just said again, one of them. So I don't know who one of them means. Your dad has a very sensitive kind of a brain. I think it is hammering rivets in all day that does it.

There are 12,000 men out of work in Middlesbrough and the Gazette says this is because we let other countries dump their steel here and the government should put tariffs on imports of steel to make it more expensive and protect our steel industry. Another thing I don't understand is reparations. Ta Ta Pet was in and he said that the Germans were made to pay for the war, that is what reparations means. But they couldn't pay so America lent them money while they got their industry going again. But now the Germans say they can't pay reparations, and if we put a tariff on their exports of steel that will make their situation worse. Work that one out. A trade union leader from the steel workers union blames private ownership of the steel industry and said that the solution to the crisis in the steel industry is public ownership. He asked what kind of music would we get if the BBC was owned by private enterprise. I don't know the answer to that one because we can't afford a wireless. I only read in the paper what's on. I know there's a famous pianist called Kreisler playing at the Corporation Hotel and I'd like to go to listen but no chance. Councillor Eckert's free concert for the unemployed is more my barrer but as your dad is working I couldn't even get into that. But they say it was packed out with about a thousand there. Sylvia would like to go to hear Kreisler as well but no chance. She's really getting on with her piano lessons. I am going to their house on Sunday to hear her practice and do her hair.

There's trouble everywhere. I've just read that there's trouble between Japan and China and there's a rebellion against the government in Spain and anarchists have declared a communist republic in a part of Spain. I will have to ask Stan Cole about it, he buys a communist paper and see what they say. I just hope we can keep out of it. Well, I don't want to finish on depressing news so did you know that the 20th of January is St Agnes Eve. I didn't know either but I have just read that it is and there's a superstition that on St Agnes Eve a maiden can find out who her future husband is if she does certain things. In County Durham they say that on St Agnes Eve a maiden must fast for 24 hours, walk upstairs to bed backwards, drink a glass full of salt water before she goes to bed, and say, "St Agnes be a friend to me, In the gift I ask of thee, Let me this night my husband see." Just think, if I had known that you mightn't have been the son of a riveter. I thought I would pull Ta Ta Pet's leg when he came in so I asked him if his wife walked upstairs backwards and all that to be warned who she was going to marry, and he started spouting poetry. Ta Ta Pet is full of surprises. You don't expect somebody to walk in wearing bicycle clips and start spouting poetry. He held his arm up in the air and started, "St Agnes Eve, ah bitter chill it was, The owl for all his feathers was a'cold." We just looked at him. He hadn't even taken his bicycle clips off. Then he looked a bit embarrassed and said it was

written by John Keats, whoever he is. Well, that's a bit more education for you. Write soon. I look forward to hearing from you if it's just a post card.
Everybody asks to be remembered.
Your everloving Mam
PS Some good news. Boro 3 West Ham 2. Something for your dad to be cheerful about.

Wednesday 27 January 1932

Dear Bob,

There's dreadful news from here and with you being in the Navy it seems personal. A submarine M2 has sunk off Portland and they can't find her. There are 56 officers and men on board. We are all keeping our fingers crossed and praying that they will be rescued. Have you heard about it? And talk about coincidence, there's a photo in the Gazette of Captain John Bell of Redcar who rammed and sank the first German submarine in the War. He's just died.

You will want to know what is happening at home. Well, the new swimming baths are nearly complete and will soon be ready for opening. Sadie and I were talking about it, and Sadie said that Jack Hatfield had swam two lengths in the new baths. Jimmy, who had his nose in the Magnet but with his ears flapping in all directions piped up. "Mam. How could Jack Hatfield swim two lengths if there was no water in the baths?" I said to Sadie, "Take no notice. It runs in the family." and she said, "Which side, yours or your ould fella's?" I gave her one of my cutting looks.

Talking about our Jimmy, we've got a new Catholic church on Linthorpe Rd. It's called the Sacred Heart and St Philomena. Well, I don't know whether it was that that started it off but Jimmy came in and said he wished he was a Catholic. So I said why, and he said because you can go and confess your sins and God lets you off. Well, our Jimmy wouldn't know what a sin was if one jumped up and bit him so I said you can confess to me if you done something wrong. Or your dad. Well he was definitely against confessing to his dad and he didn't think confessing to me left him much room for mischief. So I said well what have you done wrong and he said nothing. So I said if you've done nothing wrong there's nothing to confess to God about is there. That put him on the ropes. And that

reminded me of the time when he came in with his trouser pockets bulging. "What's in your pockets?" sez me.
"Nothing." So I looked in his pockets and got two apples out. "What's these?" I said and he looked at them as if he had never seen them before.
"Where did you get them?" says I. Sometimes our Jimmy's face reminds me of a Christmas card we got once. It was all snow and there was a five barred gate and a robin on it looking as if it was wondering what came next. "Where did you get them?"
"I don't know." he says. Then the light came on inside his head that lights his face up and you know inspiration has arrived. "They fell off a tree." he says.
"Where is this tree?" I asked.
"Limes Road." he says.
"And who was up the tree?"
"Nobody" he says, all hurt like.
"If you were confessing to God He would know who was up that tree."
That got him.
"Peter Cassidy." he said.
I might have guessed. Like father like son. His dad John was a little rascal. But he's settled down now and works on the docks. It wouldn't surprise me if it was Peter that put the idea into Jimmy's head about being a Catholic and confessing and having a clear week ahead. But I didn't ask Jimmy. Children have to have some secrets if they are going to survive in the adult world that waits for them.

The Ford American motor car company is opening a new factory at Dagenham in London that will make 200,000 cars every year. I can't imagine that number of motor cars. I asked your dad if this would mean work for the steel works here but he thinks we make the wrong kind of steel. But you never know. Your dad doesn't know everything. I'll have to ask Stan Cole. He does. I don't know why they are going to make cars here when there is so much unemployment in America. A man who was in the Labour Government has just come back from America and he says there's no dole or public assistance there at all. And we complain about the Means Test. Not that I am in favour of the Means Test, I'm not, and there's some very bitter letters in the Gazette from people giving their experiences with the Public Assistance Committee. It's very humiliating. But to have nothing at all doesn't bear thinking about.

There's been a mutiny here in Dartmoor prison with convicts and warders fighting each other. Part of the prison has been set on fire. Some of the convicts helped the warders so you wonder what the trouble is all about. I was talking to Mrs Levinson, you know the lady I clean for, about it, or she was talking to me about it while we were having a cup of tea. She says the world is a very troubled place now with the trouble in Spain, the Nazis and Communists in Germany and now the Japanese and Chinese are at it. She blames the Communists and Socialists for stirring up trouble though what that's got to do with China and Dartmoor I don't know. Between Mrs Levinson and Stan I will get an explanation. Actually two explanations. And then I'll wish I hadn't asked.

The corporation is going to build a lot of houses on the Whinney Banks and Brambles Farm so there will be a lot of work for builders. I said to your dad that this could be the end of unemployment like the sunblind theory. I told you about it in one of my letters.

There's been another pit disaster, this time in Wales. There was an explosion.

Sadie was telling me that she got Mr Muir going again. She's a real trouble maker. It was the Cleveland Scots annual Burns dinner and she was pulling his leg that she saw him in the Gazette in his kilt. He never learns. We had him the same way last year and he fell for it again.

Well that's all this time. I look forward to hearing from you soon.

Your everloving
Mam
PS Sheffield Wednesday 1 Boro 1

Tuesday 2 February 1932

Dear Bob,

We have received your letter telling us that you are at St Kitts in the West Indies. You will be having warmer weather than we are. The lake in Albert Park is frozen over.

There's some sad news from here about the submarine M2 that sank off Portland. They still can't find her and they have said that there is no hope of rescuing the crew. There are 60 men on her and that includes two RAF men. The submarine is equipped to carry a seaplane. I didn't know that submarines can carry seaplanes. Anyway the King has sent a message of sympathy to the families of the men who are lost. I hope you never volunteer for submarines. And so does Sylvia. We were talking about it. I have to tell you that she has received your letter and she will be writing.

I worry about the situation. China has declared war on Japan and they say our warships are going to China to protect British people there. And American ships. The Japanese have sent warships and more soldiers.

Things seem to be getting worse here as well. The Corporation is stopping building work that it was going to do and teachers and others who work for the Corporation have had their wages cut. A man who was in the army has a letter in the Gazette saying that he is out of work and living with his parents and because his father is working he has had his dole stopped. The MP for Stockton Mr McMillan who is a conservative says he is going to do what he can to revise the unemployment scheme. I wish him luck. The Prince of Wales has made a big speech in the Albert Hall saying there is a crisis and asking people to give of their best by personal service. Stan Cole says that he is asking us to work for nothing but I don't believe that because what would we live on. So Stan says well what does he mean and I have to say I don't know.

There's a man here who knows how to solve his crisis. He was in court for debt and he said that he was out of work so he got married to get somebody to keep him. His wife gets money off her family and she gives him two and six a week for cigarettes. The judge said he has to pay a shilling a week off his debts. Mrs Wilson and me were talking about it and she said how does he get into debt on two and six a week. She's a cracker sometimes, Mrs Wilson. She said she read in the Gazette that Middlesbrough has a white elephant. It's the new fire engine that the corporation bought. It's too big to go into the fire station so they have to pay £18.10 shillings a year to keep it in a garage and they hardly ever used it. She wanted to know what a white elephant is so I could only say it's a fire engine. I know it is more than that because I have heard about posh people having white elephant sales to help the church or something. I know there aren't any round here.

One of our magistrates has said juvenile crime is rising and he blames penny bloods or lack of control by parents. I'm going to have to watch our Jimmy.

Sadie Quinn has been reading about shares. She doesn't understand them but she knows that people own shares in companies and get dividends. So she's been cracking on to me about how she's going to start buying some. It's only a joke. Anyway the other night Ta Ta Pet arrived and no sooner had he come in than Sadie made her appearance. She told me later that she had seen Ta Ta Pet come in and she came over on impulse. I was thinking of selling my gilts and buying some shares, she said. Well I knew she would no more know what gilts are than I do. I didn't even know there's any such thing. If anybody had asked me I would have said they were pigs. So I was absolutely astonished. But that was nothing to the effect it had on Ta Ta Pet. Talking about gilts and buying shares is not something that people do round here. When he recovered his composure as they say in the novels I read he said "Why are you selling your Government stocks?" It was Sadie's turn to be surprised. She didn't know that gilts are government stocks and she didn't know what government stocks are but she couldn't say so. You have to give it to Sadie. She's not surprised for long, at least she doesn't show it. She turned her smile on Ta Ta Pet full dazzle. She's very good looking and poor old Ta Ta Pet just melted. I felt his knees giving way. I don't mean that I was feeling his knees, I just sort of felt the vibrations coming under the table if you know what I mean. "What would you advise me?" says Sadie. Ta Ta Pet croaked something about it's the wrong time to sell gilts because there is a good rate of interest and buying shares is risky. Sadie said she would take his advice and she left in a hurry.

When she'd gone Ta Ta Pet said to me he didn't think Mrs Quinn would have the money to buy gilts or shares. Well, I didn't want him to catch on that she was pulling his leg, so I said she got a legacy from Ireland. I knew I'd made a mistake the minute I said it but it was out. "Oh", says Ta Ta Pet surprised. "Who died?" Her mother I think, says I. "Oh I am sorry" says Ta Ta Pet. "Should I go over and offer my condolences?" I nearly jumped out of me skin.

"No. No. Don't do that, it was some time ago and it would only remind her. But don't tell anybody about her legacy will you?", I sez. I could feel myself getting in deeper and deeper. No. He promised. So I just have to hope that Ta Ta Pet can keep his mouth shut.

Listen to this. The Cannon Ward Women Conservatives held their annual whist drive and dance in the Assembly Rooms the other night. Conservative women down Cannon Street. I can't believe it. Your Auntie Edie lives down there in Gladstone Street. Next time she comes I'll pull her leg about the Cannon Street Women Conservatives. On second thoughts I won't. I'll get Sadie to do it. She comes from Cannon Street so I'll get her to come over and put her posh accent on and I'll watch your Auntie Edie's face.

Well, I'll have to go. The jam and bread kid is due any time now. I will keep writing. Everybody here asks to be remembered and your dad asks for his usual PS.

Your everloving

Mam

PS Boro 3 Bolton Wanderers 0. Jubilation round here

Tuesday 9 February 1932

Dear Bob,

Well, here I am again keeping you up with what is happening at home and all the local gossip as your dad calls it.

The situation in China seems to be getting worse and it looks as if we are being dragged in. HMS Kent and HMS Berwick have arrived at Shanghai and landed troops from the Argyll and Sutherland Highlanders but they must be well outnumbered. The Americans have landed troops as well. I hope the Norfolk is not going.

The submarine M2 has been found off Portland and a service has been held at sea for the men who were lost. Divers have been down trying to put wires round her to bring her to the surface. At the disarmament conference in Geneva Britain has proposed that submarines be abolished and the Americans have agreed which is a good thing, they are dreadful kinds of ships and awfully dangerous. I hope you never volunteer for them. France has proposed that the League of Nations should have an army to keep the peace. I thought that was a good idea until somebody has said that it will create a super state so I am not so sure. What do you think? We wouldn't have a Navy. Do you think your ship will be going to Cuba to help the people? There's been a terrible earthquake there.

Some merchant seamen here have gone on strike. They only get £7.15s.6d a month and the ship owners are going to cut their wages. Some of the men have formed what they call a Minority Movement and are asking the other men to leave their union and form another one because their union is not supporting them. We think we are hard up but in America some of the cities are going bankrupt. How does a city go bankrupt? Stan Cole said they are spending more than they raise in taxes and nobody will lend them money. So there you are. It won't happen here that's for sure. Our governments would get blood out of a stone.

You were asking about the boxing. His nibs is well up on that. He doesn't call that local gossip. He said that Larry Gains who is coloured was allowed to fight a South African for the empire championship because the dominion boxing rules do not stop coloured men boxing with white. The fight was a draw. But British boxing rules are that they cannot fight each other and the secretary of the British Boxing Board has said that a coloured man will never be the champion of Great Britain. Canada does not have a colour bar and that's where Larry Gains comes from, but we do and so does South Africa. I hope that answers your question. It's very complicated, isn't it? They could fight for us in the war against the Germans and win the Victoria Cross but they are not good enough to be the British boxing champion. It's like us women, we are not good enough for lots of things either.

Well, to finish off with. I told you in my last letter about Sadie coming over to pull Ta Ta Pet's leg about how she was going to sell her gilts and how that turned out and how Ta Ta Pet said to me after she had gone that he didn't know Sadie had money to buy shares. And how I explained that she had got a legacy when her mother died and I only made it up so he wouldn't know that Sadie had been pulling his leg. And he promised not to tell anybody.

Well, yesterday your dad came in from Stan Cole's shed for his dinner. We just sat down and got started when your dad says I hear Mrs Quinn has inherited a legacy. Her mother over in Ireland died. I nearly choked. What's the matter, he said. Nothing, I said. A bit of suet pudding went down the wrong way that's all. Then I said I don't believe that story. If Sadie got a legacy she would have told me. Well Paddy's kept very quiet about it as well, says your dad, although he never says much so maybe they're both keeping it quiet.

Then Jimmy put in his two pennorth. Mam, what's a legacy? Nothing for you to worry about, sez me. I'll tell you another time. Why not now he says. Little boys should be seen and not heard I said. I didn't like shutting him up like that but somehow I had to try to protect Sadie from her legacy.

Later, after your dad had gone out, Sadie came over. "You'll never believe this," she says, "Mrs Walters came in and asked me for the lend of a pound. I thought she was joking so I said a pound of what. And she said, no, a pound in money." She wanted to buy some clothes for the kids. She seemed serious. So I said, well I don't have money like that and she said she wouldn't have asked but she'd heard about my legacy. I said what legacy and she went quiet. I think somebody put her up to it or she was pulling my leg. Unless there's something wrong with her. I've noticed she seemed a bit funny lately. I had to agree.

Later on Mrs Turner called in and she asked me if I had heard that Sadie's mother had died. I didn't know what to say, so I said not really. And she said "What do you mean? You haven't really heard or she hasn't really died?" I could feel myself getting drawn further and further in, so I said well I'm sure that if Sadie's mother had died, she would have told me. I meant Sadie, not her mother. So Mrs Turner said well what about her legacy. I could have strangled Ta Ta Pet.

When Ta Ta Pet came in for his insurance money I asked him if he told anybody about Sadie's mother dying and leaving Sadie a legacy. Fortunately your dad wasn't in otherwise I couldn't have asked. Anyway Ta Ta Pet sez no he hadn't told anybody so I sez how is it that people are talking about it. Then he looked thoughtful and he said well, maybe he had told Mrs Turnbull when she gave him a glass of her rhubarb wine. Just one glass, I said. Well maybe it was more than one but he couldn't remember if it was one or two. Well if Ta Ta Pet couldn't remember if he had one glass or two he definitely had two. The first glass goes to your knees. It's the second glass that does the real damage. So that's where it started. Now everybody in Sunnyside knows about Sadie's legacy, except Sadie. And Paddy of course, but she wouldn't have told him anyway, he would only have gambled it.

Well that's all this time. Sylvia called. She got your letter and asked me to say how pleased she was and will be writing back. Jimmy says he wants to be remembered.

Tara for now

Your everloving

Mam

PS Derby 5 Boro 2 Your dad said I had to be sure to tell you that the Boro played with only ten men in the second half because one of our players was injured.

Monday 15 February 1932

Dear Bob,

Thinking of an original start for a letter each time is a problem. So how about the weather for a change? There is snow on Roseberry Topping? That's the best that I can do. Now I can tell you something that I wanted to tell you. Sadie brought the Gazette over to show me a photograph of a South Bank boy called Wilf Mannion. He's only 13 and he's the captain of St Peter's school football team and he's been picked to play in the North versus Midlands International trial match and to play for Yorkshire against Durham. His parents must be very proud of him. Sadie is as well because St Peter's is a Catholic school. Compare what that boy is doing with the boys who are stealing these days. Somebody is blaming the shops for putting their goods on open counters where the boys give in to temptation and on automatic machines but I say that's no excuse, the blame belongs to the boys and their parents should be dealing with them. You might see big changes in Middlesbrough when you come home. Posters are going up everywhere saying shop at Middlesbrough because we are the ideal shopping centre. And the new bridge at Newport is going up fast.

HMS York has arrived home from the West Indies where you are now. The papers say that one of their stokers died of spotted fever and was buried in Trinidad. It must be very distressing for his family with the ship coming home and knowing he is not with it.

Sadie has had some bad news as well, though not as bad as that. The government has refused to give the corporation more money to complete the trunk road to Redcar and so Paddy who was working on it has been paid off. There's an advert in the Gazette saying why married women lose their looks. They say household cares are the cause and the cure is to drink three glasses of Wincarnis wine a day. How three glasses of Wincarnis will get rid of Sadie's household cares and how she could afford to pay for the Wincarnis is Sadie's problem. And the rest of us of course. And there's another one for Clubs cigarettes. 5 for 2d. Send in 50 empty packets and get a free cap. Somebody will be daft enough to fall for it, but not in this house they won't.

Ta Ta Pet was in and was telling us Edgar Wallace who writes the crime stories has died in Hollywood. He was born in London and he only went to elementary school. How some people get on with that kind of start in life is amazing but I suppose he must have had a natural talent for writing, like yours truly, sez me. And then you read about a girl in India who is a university student who has tried to shoot the Governor. Fortunately she failed and she's been sent to prison for nine years. She says she did it for her country but Mr Gandhi wants independence for India and advises people that killing is the wrong way to go about it. It's an awful waste of that girl's life. I don't know what her parents must think.

The news from Germany is strange as well. They've been talking about it in Stan Cole's shed and your dad has been keeping me up with what goes on. He's the strong silent type always with his nose in his dictionary but even he can't read his dictionary while he's having his dinner. There's too many pages and it keeps closing.

The German government says everybody should disarm because Germany is disarmed but a secret order from Herr Hitler to his party members says that when the Nazis get power which they expect to do next month he will tear up a copy of the Versailles Treaty and burn it in public and then they will march on Berlin. How do I know, if it's a secret? Because I have a spy in Stan Cole's shed, your dad, and they know. The Treaty of Versailles, in case you don't know, says me throwing me chest out, is the Treaty all the countries signed at the end of the war and says that Germany can only have a small army.

There's a big argument going on here about whether we should re-arm. I didn't know we had disarmed but Mrs Levinson doesn't trust Hitler and says if he gets power we will need a modern army and navy and I agreed with her and then your granddad told me that the Liberal MP here Kingsley Griffiths said that we are spending £200 a minute on preparation for war. I was horrified but then I remembered that I don't trust Kingsley Griffiths. He voted against putting tariffs on goods coming into Britain from abroad that are not made in the Empire and I support tariffs. We'll never get work here without them.

You were asking about boxing. There's an up and coming Middlesbrough boxer called Alf Craster has just won another fight and Len Harvey is Britain's middle weight champion. That's all I know until his nibs tells me more.

Remember I told you in my last letter about the Cannon Street Women Conservatives and how I would get Sadie to pull your Auntie Edie's leg next time she came. Well, she came on Thursday and Sadie came over and started chatting away in her posh accent about how she used to live down Cannon

Street and was in the Cannon Ward Conservative Women's Association. Well, your Auntie Edie was taking it all in and it was taking me all my time to keep my face straight. Eventually Sadie said she had some washing hanging out to dry and she'd better go and get it in.

Well, you should have heard your Auntie Edie after Sadie had gone. "Is that woman a bit touched?" she said. Sadie a bit touched, says me in surprise. No, she's all there. "Is she a fallen woman then?" says your Aunt Edie. Your Aunt Edie talks like that. She reads the women's magazines. I said "What on earth makes you think that?" "Well, a posh accent like that and living down Cannon Street.". "No", I said, "She's very religious. Goes to confession every week". "There you are then, that's it," says Edie, "they do. What's she got to confess about living round here with a garden and a bathroom?"

I can never tell Sadie what Edie said. I'll have to make something up like I didn't know you had such posh neighbours. That'll please Sadie and make her laugh.

Sylvia was in and I asked her when her birthday is, you know how nosey I am and she said it's 28th February. I'm telling you in good time so don't forget to send her a card.

Mrs Callender has just walked by in her fox fur. Those two are inseparable. See where jealousy gets you.

That's all for this time. Sadie, Ta Ta Pet, Sylvia and all round here ask to be remembered. Not forgetting Jimmy and your dad.

Your everloving,
Mam
PS Huddersfield 1 Boro 1

Monday 22 February 1932

Dear Bob,

Because it's cold here I was nearly going to tell you not to forget to wrap up warm. Then I remembered where you are. Being as you are in that direction I wonder if you hear what is going on in America. We are told the big cities there are going bankrupt. Mrs Muir told me they'd been discussing it in Stan Cole's shed and I don't like to think that Mrs Muir knows more than me so I asked your dad how a city could go bankrupt. Sometimes your dad overdoes the strong silent type, sitting with his nose in his dictionary and keeping me dangling when he knows I want to know something, and acting as if thumbscrews wouldn't get a word out of him. But finally he caved in. Chicago has been in court arguing for nearly two years if their tax assessments are legal. And while the arguing has been going on people have not been paying their taxes. So teachers and other employees have only been getting a part of their wages. There's big trouble in Chicago. Detroit and Philadelphia have had to cut wages and New York has cut relief for 750,000 unemployed. I just can't believe the figures but your dad said it's in black and white, although Stan Cole says you can't believe anything you read in the papers except when they agree with Stan. Apparently the only big city that is not in trouble is Milwaukee which is a stronghold of socialism. They ended the year with £800,000 in the bank. I'm a bit suspicious of that because the Americans have dollars not pounds. But wouldn't you have thought that your dad would have come rushing home from Stan Cole's shed to tell me that? Instead he comes in, flops down in the chair, and all you see is his legs and arms sticking out of that dictionary or if he has a paper you see eight fingers and his feet. I looked over the top of his paper the other day and rather than talk to me he was reading an advertisement. "How men can keep young". Take Beechams Pills.

I was talking to Mrs Wilson at the bottom shops about the unemployment situation and she said, "You know May, I admire you, you know so much." Well I gave myself a little pat on the back but you don't like to boast so I played it modest and said thank you but not really. When she'd gone, I thought how much do I know. One day in the week I have your dad at me and so I'm Labour. Another day I have Stan Cole at me so I'm nearly a Communist. Another day I have Mrs Levinson at me so I'm a Conservative. And last but not least your granddad has a go at me so I'm a Liberal. That's four days in the week. The other three I'm confused. And then they ask me to choose a government. French women have just got the right to vote for their members of Parliament. I wish them luck.

Sadie's a character. There's a photo in the Gazette taken at the undertakers' annual dance. Ta Ta Pet was in talking about the importance of insurance in case the bread winner dies and for some reason he brought the undertakers' dance into it and he said to Sadie, "You know the undertakers' dance?" and Sadie said "No, how does it go?" I couldn't help laughing and poor old Ta Ta Pet just stood there looking totally lost when who walks in but your Auntie Edie. Sadie's face when she saw Edie was a study because she knew that Edie had heard her.

Edie's face was a study as well because not only did she now know that Sadie did not have a posh accent but she must have been putting it on for Edie's benefit last week. And more than that, she knew that I knew. I could see the numbers going round in your Aunt Edie's head and she was getting two and two and there's one thing you can say about our Edie and that is that she's good at arithmetic. "Hello," she sez to Sadie, "how's the Conservative Women's Association getting on?" Ta Ta Pet looked at Sadie and there was a look in his eye that was saying legacy, shares, Conservative Women's Association, insurance. Sadie couldn't know that of course because she didn't know about her legacy. But I knew that Ta Ta Pet was in for a disappointment and I was in for whatever Edie had in store for me when the others had gone. I began to feel sorry for myself.

Well, after the other two had gone Edie started on me but she couldn't keep it up for long. After all we are sisters and we used to fight when we were young and lived down Carlow Street. So suddenly she saw the funny side of it and she started to laugh. "You don't change, do you?" she said. I don't know what she meant by that. I've been reading the advert, "What makes married women lose their good looks". Well I know what they said but three glasses of Wincarnis a day isn't going to bring them back. Not that I've lost mine of course.

There are interesting letters in the Gazette about the history of Middlesbrough. There's one in about Cargo Fleet. Centuries ago it was Caldecotes and that became Caldcotes. Then that became Calcoat Fleet. Mr Askew who wrote the letter says that cald meant cold in old English and cotes meant cottages and fleet meant a creek, inlet or estuary so Cargo Fleet only meant cold cottages on the creek. I expect somebody will write in saying he's got it all wrong, they usually do.

News on the boxing is that Alf Craster the Boro middleweight has been winning a lot of fights so your dad says he is somebody who may be going places. And you will be pleased to know that Middlesbrough beer is the strongest going. It's good to have something to be proud of.

I've been saving our bad news till last. Furness's shipyard have launched a ship, SS Remola and your dad's been paid off. And Middlesbrough Public Assistance Committee are boasting that by disallowing a lot of claims for assistance they are saving over £1,000 a week. If they find out that I have a little cleaning job for Mrs Levinson we will be in for it as well. But I suppose our bad luck is not as bad as China where the

Japanese are shelling and bombing and dead bodies of Chinese men, women and children are lying out in the streets. God knows where it will all end.

Well, I will have to go, Jimmy's in for a slice of jam and bread and asks to be remembered.

Your everloving
Mam.

PS The silver lining through the clouds. The Boro drew with Huddersfield on Wednesday one each and on Saturday beat Newcastle 2-1. Smiling faces all round.

Monday 29 February 1932

Dear Bob,

You really are a chip off the old block. You write and tell us that you are in Trinidad and you don't tell us a thing about what it's like or what you do there. You tell us you have been to St Kitts, Charleston, Dominica, Barbados, all these places and the furthest I have been is Redcar. Still it's nice to have a son who is seeing all these places so that I feel as if I am visiting them. You can tell us all about it when you come on leave.

Yesterday was Sylvia's birthday so I baked a birthday cake and Jimmy painted a birthday card for her and we invited Sylvia and her mother round for tea. I made some sandwiches that I read about in a detective story that the posh people have and when I was drinking my tea I crooked my little finger and held it up in the air just to show Sylvia's mother that her daughter is mixing with a good family. Sylvia cut the cake and we all sang happy birthday and Sylvia and her mother took the rest of the cake home.

More on the history of Middlesbrough from readers' letters in the Gazette. I wonder if any of them went to Archibald School like I did. Anyway I've never thought about why the Longlands is called the Longlands or why Breckon Hill Road is called that name but there were monks' cells centuries ago and a man named John de Longland had land at Longlands and John de Breckon had land at Breckon Hill and the monks wrote it down. You don't think of Middlesbrough having history like that. We only get told that there was a farm house in 1824 and they can't even agree whether there was one or two. And there's another letter saying that Caldecotes was a village in Ormesby and the sea used to come right up to it and to Clay Lane Steelworks before the river was dredged and an embankment and the breakwater built. I always wondered why

Eston Nab was called a nab. After all it's just a brick building. But it comes from the Saxon word kneap meaning nab or summit. Climbing up there will never be the same again.

We're even getting a different story now about how the ironstone was discovered that started Middlesbrough off as an iron and steel town. I always thought someone was out walking on Eston Hills and kicked a stone and realised it was ironstone. But I was on my hands and knees ready to light the fire when I read in the Gazette that it wasn't like that at all. I tell you I'm absolutely bursting with knowledge. In fact it was found on the beach at Huntcliff and the man who found it was with a man who owned land at Skinningrove and he gave permission for the ironstone to be dug up if he was paid 6d a ton. Later on the right to dig it up was sold for two glasses of brandy to a man who sold the stone to Bolckow Vaughans. I wonder if Ta Ta Pet knows that. I'll ask him. He probably does and if he didn't he will say that he did.

Do you remember Chief Petty Officer Willis who saved a lot of lives when the submarine Poseidon went down? He left the Navy because of ill health. Well, the King has just presented him with the Albert Medal for bravery.

There's a shortage of nurses here. They say it is because they have to pay a £5 deposit which they lose if they leave before their three years training is finished and they have to buy their own uniform. The bosses don't make things easy for people. And yet they need trained people.

The news from China is frightening. Japanese aeroplanes from aircraft carriers have destroyed all the Chinese aeroplanes and we have warships gong there. And parts of Hangchow are in flames. It worries me that it might come here. We read all the time about people trying to break speed records. Sir Malcolm Campbell has just driven a motor car at over 242 miles an hour. At the same time that you feel proud that it is an Englishman that has done it it makes you wonder where he thinks he is going to at that speed. You wouldn't be allowed to drive down the road like that. Mr Wells, you know he is an engine driver and big union man, was telling us that there is trouble on the railways. It is cheaper to send goods by road than by rail so that is what is happening and the railway companies are complaining that they are losing business. And they are saying that they have to pay taxes to build roads, so they say that the Government should help them. The union is worried because it could lead to unemployment on the railway. Mr Wells says that the way Hitler in Germany talks he thinks that if Hitler gets power we will have another war. The Russians are saying that the disarmament talks in Geneva are a cover up for the capitalist countries who want a war against Russia. I don't understand that at all. If our country is proposing disarmament how can that be a cover up? But if they are right and we go to war we will need the railways to carry all the men and munitions and the roads could never do it. Listening to Mr Wells talking like that makes me worry because he is no hothead. He doesn't go in Stan Cole's shed but he is a big union man and very serious.

To change the subject. How about this from America? A man broke into a flat where two sisters lived and said he wanted their jewels. They were worth a thousand pounds but they said they had sentimental value so he said he would leave them if they would give him £100 in cash. Anyway they beat him down to £20 and they think they got a bargain because they saved £980. And the ice cream man Mr Rea has been fined a shilling for selling ice cream on a Sunday on the Whinney Banks estate. His excuse was that he thought that the Whinney Banks were outside Middlesbrough. As the old Yorkshire saying goes, There's nowt so queer as folk.

Well Bob, that's all for this time. Everybody asks to be remembered. Write soon.

Your everloving
Mam

PS Boro 0 Blackpool 3

Monday 7 March 1932

Dear Bob,

How are you? My usual question I know but I do think of you a lot which is natural and hope that everything is fine with you. I know that you are having better weather than we are so that's something. It can't be good at sea in bad weather. We were talking about the Navy when Ta Ta Pet was in. He said he had read that the Government has ordered another three cruisers and some destroyers and sloops. Will you explain the difference when you write. Your dad said cruisers are bigger than destroyers and have bigger guns but that's as much as he knows and Ta Ta Pet doesn't know either which is unusual for him. They've also ordered three submarines and yet our Government has proposed that submarines should be outlawed at the disarmament talks. Do you know the cruiser

HMS Emerald. A petty officer has fallen overboard and drowned. They got his body back and he's been buried in Iraq. That's going to be a tragedy for some poor souls here at home.

Mrs Levinson was talking about the order for more ships as well. She is in favour of a bigger navy but she said that we are going to spend less this year on the navy than before. Mrs Levinson is pretty knowledgeable about these things which I suppose you can understand because she talks to MPs and business people. She was on about the war in China where the Japanese are advancing against the Chinese and how our government is trying to get them to agree to end the war. I was telling your dad what she said and he said they'd been discussing it in Stan Cole's shed and Stan had said that we are helping the Japanese by selling them arms. We've sold them over £200,000 worth and sold only £45,000 to the Chinese. You wonder how governments can do things like that, the poor Chinese are being killed and probably with guns we sold to the Japanese and at the same time our Government is supposed to be trying to stop the fighting. Stan says it's all done for profit, but Stan would say that.

You will see some changes when you come home. The beck for one. You know the beck used to flood, the Palladium, Deepdale, all the way down the back of Albert Park to North Ormesby crossing. Well the council has been building concrete walls along the sides of the beck from Emmerson Ave down to the back of the park to prevent it flooding again and they are nearly finished. It's given work to a lot of men but now they will be paid off so there will be more unemployed though the Corporation are going to build a lot of houses on the Whinney Banks so that will provide some work. The Gazette says that there have been two million houses built since the war and the Government should now start demolishing the slums.

Dixons' shipyard near the transporter where your dad used to work is going to be auctioned off. The King and Queen visited the yard during the war. Your dad wasn't there then of course he was in the army. Storm Jameson wrote about the yard in two novels, The Lonely Ship and The Voyage Home. I haven't read them, in fact I didn't know they existed but Bertie Gibson, you know, the head lad in the Sons of Temperance was telling me. He's pretty well up on these things. He does a lot of reading. In fact I wouldn't be surprised if he is one of these anonymous letter writers to the Gazette.

Sadie's still got a bee in her bonnet about shares. I've tried to talk her out of it but she just says, well, Paddy gambles on the horses so why shouldn't she buy and sell shares. I said that Paddy has money to put on horses but she doesn't have any money to buy shares with. But she just says it's harmless and something to do so I leave her to get on with it.

Anyway the other night she came across the road to our house and started on about shares. She said she had seen in the Gazette that Binns' profits are up and their preference shares had paid a dividend of 10% and their ordinary shares had paid a dividend of 20%. She said she was thinking of buying some but she didn't know the difference between preference and ordinary so she asked your dad what the difference is. Well your dad doesn't know anything about shares, he knows how to run the country but that's different. So he said he didn't know but Ta Ta Pet probably would because he's an insurance man. Sadie of course is only joking and she thinks that your dad knows she's only joking but she doesn't know that your dad thinks she's got a legacy so he thinks she's serious. Did I tell you that I tried to persuade your dad that the story that Sadie had got a legacy couldn't be true because her mother couldn't be dead because she had written to Sadie only the previous week. Your dad said that was not possible because Sadie's mother couldn't read and write. He said that Paddy had told him that some time ago. So I said somebody else wrote the letter for her and she put her cross on it. Your dad gave me one of those old fashioned looks that say you're lying, I know you're lying but I don't know why you're lying. Which of course I was. Well, not really, I only made it up to protect Sadie. So I changed the subject before he had time to wonder how I could think that Sadie's mother had written to her if she couldn't read and write and anyway she was dead. This story that I made up about Sadie's mother dying and leaving her a legacy is going to end up in tears, mine, and I only did it to help Sadie. You see what comes of being a good Samaritan.

Talking about what your dad doesn't know about shares he didn't even know we pay rates so naturally I didn't know either but Ta Ta Pet was saying that the rates are being reduced this year and when I said it didn't matter to me because we don't pay rates he said we do but we pay it with our rent. You learn something every day.

Do you remember about Colonel Lindbergh the American who flew the Atlantic in 1927. Well his baby has been kidnapped and the kidnappers have asked for £10,000 ransom money. What a wicked thing to do. The American gangster Al Capone has said that if they will let him out of prison he will look for the baby. The idea is that the gangsters will be able to find out who did it but I can't see the American Government letting him out. There seems to be trouble everywhere you look. Now they are at it in Finland where the Fascist Revolutionary Party has seized control of some towns and are threatening to march on the capital. Stan Cole says they are the same crowd as Hitler in Germany and Mussolini in Italy. It seems like they are linking up.

Well some good news to end on. A Middlesbrough man Cyril Smith who plays the piano is a big success in London so that's putting Middlesbrough on the map and it should be encouragement to Sylvia. She's still sticking at it where so many start with good intentions but give up because it is too much like hard work and it takes lots of practice. And in the letters page somebody who signs himself Sympathy has written that no one thinks of the poor wives who are the real bearers of the present burden. I know what he means and we will say amen to that round here. Although I don't think Mrs Levinson has much of a burden though she is good to me. Your dad and me are going to the Palladium to see Hobson's Choice which is a comedy.

Well Bob, I must go and take up the burden again.

Your everloving

Mam

Monday 14 March 1932

Dear Bob,

Just to let you know that your letter arrived. Welcome home to England and we are looking forward to you coming home on leave. Meantime I will keep on doing what I enjoy doing so much, writing to you and letting you know everything that is going on. It is really the highlight of my week.

Mrs Levinson has asked me to do for her for another two hours a week which is good news for us. I think she wants me because I am intelligent, hard working and good looking. Well, if I don't say so who will? Anyway she asked me if I would like another two hours and of course I jumped at the chance. Then she asked me if I would like to help the Conservative Women's Association at their sale of second hand clothes to raise money for the Conservative Party. Well, to quote that old saying that I've just made up, when somebody offers you roses watch out for the thorns. But what choice did I have. Refusing was not really a choice. It was like when your dad gave me some roses that he'd picked up Donkey Lane. That was before we got married. The thorns came later. He's a canny lad though really so I'm not complaining. I'll say this for him, he always asks me for money not like some men I could name in this town who always take it off their wives. But he's not pleased about me helping at the Conservative women's fund raising, but as I said to him there are Labour MPs in the Government that he keeps complaining about so what's the difference. Anyway he's not opposed to the extra money I will get. You can't have it both ways in this life, that's a lesson I learned long ago.

There's a lot of talk going on here, in this house I mean and Stan Cole's shed about the election results for the President of Germany on the first ballot. I didn't know what they were talking about at first but your dad and Ta Ta Pet explained it. The German system isn't like ours. They elect a President while we have a king and to be elected the President has to get more than half of the votes. If nobody does then they have a second ballot. Anyway nobody got more than half of the votes though it was near. President Hindenburg got over 13 millions, Hitler got over 11 millions, the communist got nearly 5 millions and then there was somebody else with nearly 3 millions. So there we are and we have to wait to see what happens next. Mrs Levinson was saying that some people are relieved at the result because they were afraid that Hitler would get in. Stan Cole said he never had a chance of winning.

There's a lot of argument going on in the papers about the League of Nations and whether it is a good thing or whether we should be arming ourselves ready for another war. That's terrible. It is only 14 years since the last one and we are talking about another. Somebody has said in the Gazette that we are spending one thousand pounds a minute on arms and here we are struggling to make ends meet. The government is cutting wages and salaries and allowances for the unemployed and bring in a Means Test and yet they can spend all that money on guns. There's a man here just been disallowed the dole because he won £125 in a competition two years ago and he said that he still does competitions so the umpire has said that entering competitions is an occupation so as he is working he can't have the dole. Did you ever here anything so crack pot and cruel. I'm sure God must look down on us and think we are mad. And the advertisements go on about how to cure housewives whose nerve fails. I can tell them the answer to that one and it isn't taking Dr William's Pink Pills or drinking three glasses of Wincarnis every day. It's enough to give you a nervous breakdown just thinking about where the money's coming from to buy those so called cures.

The argument about whether we should put a tax on imports to protect our industry goes on. The editor of the Gazette says that our blast furnaces are obsolete and tariffs on imports should not be protection for the inefficient. There's other arguments as well, it's enough to drive you to drink trying to make sense of all the arguments that are going on.

Sadie's a laugh she really is. She came in and said I see you've got your best table cloth on, it was a copy of the Gazette and she sat down and started reading it in that posh voice that she puts on. I see Dickson and Benson's are having a mannequin parade she said. And they have new corsets fitted with Twilfit spiral steel, non rusting, unbreakable and delightfully flexible. If there's anything that I need right now she said it's a pair of corsets that won't go rusty. And so she went on. Then she started on about how she was going to ask Paddy to take her to the Hippodrome to see The Great Lover and she asked your dad if he was going to see it. She's a real mischief maker. I want to go to the Elite to see Warner Oland who usually plays Charlie Chan the Chinese detective and Anna May Wong in Daughter of the Dragon. Then Jimmy piped up, "Mam what's a great lover". I was still trying to think of an answer to that when Sadie said it's somebody who likes cigarette cards. So then he wanted to know if he was a great lover because he likes cigarette cards. So I said no it's only grown ups who like cigarette cards. So then Jimmy said our dad collects cigarette cards so is he a great lover. I saw Sadie's face become very interested and your dad disappeared further behind his dictionary. I said no, your dad collects cigarette cards to send away to get a picture to hang on the wall like the Boyhood of Raleigh there on our wall. Well, that shut Jimmy up and I thought that was the end of it and sighs of relief all round when in walked Ta Ta Pet and straightaway our Jimmy asked him if he was a great lover. I thought Ta Ta Pet was going to choke so I explained to him about the cigarette cards and he said he only collected cigarette cards when he was a boy and

Jimmy was satisfied with that. But he does ask awkward questions.

Stan Cole is over the moon. Somebody he knows called Mr Hillary Brown who lives in Southfield Road is going to Russia for two years to work on the editorial staff of Moscow News. What good that does Stan I don't know but he is really pleased about it.

The result of the election by the miners of their new leader has been announced. It's a man called Ebby Edwards from Northumberland. He went down the mines when he was twelve. When he was 23 he won a scholarship to Ruskin College in Oxford and when he finished there he went back down the mines. Just imagine that, leaving school at 12 then going to Oxford then going back down the mines when he could have got a good job with that education. I think a man like that is to be admired and he deserved to be elected.

Well Bob, I'll have to go. We all look forward to seeing you soon.

Your everloving
Mam
PS Boro 0 Sunderland 1

Wednesday 30 March 1932

Dear Bob,

Well, it was grand to have you home for Easter but it passed much too quickly. Now I have to say we are looking forward to your next leave. I was reading in one of the old Gazettes that our fish and chips were wrapped in about the battle cruiser HMS Repulse coming home from where you were and the battleship Malaya being caught in a very bad gale. What's the difference between a battle cruiser and a battleship.

The future is looking bad for shipbuilding here with the shipyards being auctioned off. Stan Cole was livid the price they've been going for, a crane for example 55 shillings. Machinery which cost £2,250 sold for £60. Yet we have to pay 16 guineas for a wireless set. Not that we will be buying one. We could buy one on the never never but your dad says out of debt out of danger but I say what danger, if we can't keep up the payments they will only come and take the wireless set back but your dad says yes and we lose all the money we paid. We seem to be helpless while somebody is making lots of money.

I decided to try to put an end to the story that Sadie has a legacy so I asked Ta Ta Pet to tell Mrs Turnbull that he was wrong when he told her that Sadie's mother had died and left her a legacy. So he said why should he do that when it was me who was his source. So I said because I had got it wrong, it was actually somebody else who died and left a legacy to somebody else but I got the names mixed up. He wasn't a bit keen because he hadn't told Mrs Turnbull that I had told him and it would look like he got it wrong but he said he would do it if he could tell Mrs Turnbull where he got the story from in the first place. Well, I couldn't have that because once Mrs Turnbull starts talking it will get back to Sadie that I had said that her mother had died and left her a legacy. When I could see that I wasn't getting anywhere with Ta Ta Pet I decided to lose my rag and put on my stern look. I do it with your dad sometimes not that he takes any notice. I get somewhere sometimes if I whisper sweet nothings in his ear. But I can't try that on Ta Ta Pet, I'm not married to him although sometimes I look at his bicycle clips and get ideas that are probably above my station. He took them off once and laid them on our table and I could see they had Made in England stamped on them. Probably Sheffield steel as well. Sadie told me once that her silver has Sheffield steel stamped on it. It was a wedding present. Not as good as Middlesbrough though but we build bridges with our steel.

There's a row going on here about the means test. The Borough Treasurer has reported to the Public Assistance Committee that some grocers are supplying goods on relief tickets that are not on the specified list like fancy biscuits, tinned fruit, bottles of pickles, shredded wheat, and cigarettes. The shop assistants say that if they don't give the customers these things they would only go to another shop. One of the Aldermen on the committee said that a lot of people who are not on relief can't afford these things and the shops that are doing it should be suspended from the scheme for a few months. Canon Sullivan asked if more relief could not be given in cash but another said that if it was a lot of it would be spent on beer instead of food. But the treasurer said that 90% of our relief already is given in cash. The committee said that there are more people than ever claiming the dole or relief but by reducing the amounts they have allowed a to lot of people and not allowing some at all to others they are saving £1,340 a week. The Gazette says that people who have used up the weeks they are entitled to on the dole then get public charity and the means test is to make sure that those who claim are genuine. That makes me feel bad because I work for Mrs Levinson although we couldn't live on what she pays me but it would be stopped off us if I told them so I just have to feel bad and hope and pray that they don't find out.

You remember the submarine M2 that sank off Portland. A diver has recovered the body of a leading seaman from the hangar. He was only 28 and had been in the navy fourteen years.

Well, the Sydney Bridge has been opened and just as the Australian Prime Minister was going to cut the tape an officer in the Hussars on horseback rushed up and cut the tape with his sword. He was pulled off his horse and arrested and it turns out he is a member of a fascist organisation called the New Guard. These fascists are all over the place. It's a proud moment for us in Middlesbrough. I was reading that in 1829 six Quakers bought the site for Middlesbrough, that's where the name the Middlesbrough Owners comes from, I'd often wondered about that, and the first house was built the next year and here we are building the Sidney Bridge and bridges all over the place. It's funny reading about the post in those days. A man has been giving a lecture and he says that the penny post was introduced in May 1840 and letters to people in Middlesbrough were displayed in the office window of the Tees Coal Company and people would congregate round the window while somebody who could read would read out the names and addresses on the envelopes. It must be awful not to be able to read and write. You are at everybody's mercy. Your old school Hugh Bell has just got a new headmaster, Mr Evans who is coming from a school in Stoke. That's where your granddad and grandma come from. He came to work in the steel works and they got the house in Carlow Street that you used to go to.

It was nice of Sylvia to let me and your dad go to the Palladium with you both to see James Cagney and Joan Blondell in Larceny Lane. It was like a family outing. Well Bob, that's enough for this time. Everybody asks to be remembered.

Your everloving
Mam

PS. Your dad's just come in with his acid drops. Manchester City 1 Boro 2 and Joe Green was knocked out by Pat Gorman whoever he is. And Cambridge won the boat race. Your dad's beginning to take liberties. The agreement that I said he could have was that he could put the football results in a PS. Now look what he's getting in.

Sunday 3 April 1932

Dear Bob,

Here we are again. It's very quiet here, your dad's in bed fast asleep. I can hear him snoring. He was out with Sam Maynard last night with the nets so we have a few rabbits. The news gets around fast because I have just seen Mrs Masterman going to Sam's house carrying an empty carrier bag and when she came out it looked as if there was something in it. It's not that I'm nosey, I just happened to be looking out the window, but I need to know what's going on in the avenue. Don't forget I asked you the difference between a battleship and a battle cruiser will you. Ta Ta Pet is keen to know so he can show off his knowledge in other people's houses.

Ta Ta Pet was in when who comes walking in but Sadie and Stan together. Then Bertie Gibson arrived, you know the head lad of the Sons of Temperance. He was only wanting to see your dad about some plants for the garden but Stan never believes in missing an opportunity. It was a right ould shindig. Straight away he asks Bertie what he thinks of prohibition in America. He knows what Bertie thinks of prohibition in America, he's in favour, but he knew he'd get a reaction. Bertie can't resist a challenge especially when he's got an audience and he got on to the evils of drink. So then Stan took a side swipe at Sadie and asked Bertie what he thought of holy wine. That brought Sadie in at full speed. She got on about Jesus and the son of God and righteousness and the evils of drink. So Stan just to give the pot another stir said "As Karl Marx said, religion is the opium of the masses." Stan often quotes somebody to prove he's right. Bertie didn't agree with that. He said drink is the opium of the masses and Sadie thinks religion is essential because it teaches people about right and wrong and we get our ideas about right and wrong from God. What happens here on earth is all God's will. So then Stan said is it God's will that there is mass unemployment in the world and an MP who's just come back from America said there's no dole or relief there just soup kitchens. That had Sadie stumped but Ta Ta Pet came to her rescue. He said that God has given people free will and they make the choices between right and wrong, not God. I've heard that Ta Ta Pet goes to night classes though he never lets on. So Stan said in that case if it's not God that created unemployment it's people. And since nobody in this house or in this street closes the steelworks and the shipyards down it must be somebody else and there's only the capitalists left. I'd wondered when Stan would bring the capitalists into it. And then he brought in his clincher. Karl Marx said workers of the world unite, you have nothing to lose but your chains. Sadie wondered if Stan says that in his sleep but apart from that it was silence, the one thing they were not going to do for sure was unite, so I said who would like a cup of tea.

That broke the ice. Sadie said she didn't she had to go but she had the last word. As she went through the door she turned round and said, I must be right because there's a God, and then she was gone. Ta Ta Pet got his insurance money, Stan was speechless and Bertie talked to your dad about plants for the garden. Stan left just after them. I don't know what Jimmy made of it all because he just sat on the mat and didn't say anything. But when they'd all gone I asked your dad what he thought of it and he said "interesting". There's one thing you can say about your dad, he's a man of few words and he makes every one count.

Talking about God, the Prime Minister Ramsay MacDonald is absolutely hated round here. Up in county Durham the Fishburn miners lodge has taken his picture off their banner and put on one of the miners leader who died, A.J.Cook and they've put on the words: "The living may deceive, but the dead will never". That's one in the eye for MacDonald. Twelve shipyards have closed in the past three years mostly in Scotland and the North East so there's no love lost.

There's trouble with the Irish Government. They are going to do away with the oath to the King and refuse to pay some payments they are supposed to make. I asked Sadie what she thought of the Irish Prime Minister Mr de Valera and she said he isn't even Irish. With a name like that how could he be. She said he was born in America with a Spanish father and his mother was born in America although her parents were Irish. So how could he be Irish instead of Spanish or American. She thinks that Ireland should stay with us and I agree with her. The Gazette says that if they leave the British Empire Ireland will be a foreign country and they will lose the preference they get on their trade with Britain.

It is really strange what goes on in America. They are all immigrants really just like we are here in Middlesbrough. The only people who belong there are the Indians. In America I mean, not Middlesbrough. There's some gangsters there who had their headquarters robbed and they thought another gangster with an Italian name knew who did it. But as they say in the paper he refused to squeak so they took him for a ride and bumped him off. I've never heard anything like it.

There's a letter in the Gazette from a man in Ontario in Canada saying don't send any more lads out to Canada. There's no jobs and he's seen lines two miles long of men waiting for free meals. And I've had my weekly lecture from Mrs Levinson. I always know when there's a lecture coming up she calls me her dear. Did you know that we have a budget surplus of £364,000. Put that in your pipe and smoke it. She wrote it down for me to show my friends. She meant Stan Cole. I sometimes tell her what Stan has said. Of course Stan didn't think this was great at all, he just said that was because they are cutting wages and the dole and everything that the workers need. Stan doesn't lose a trick. I wished he worked for Mrs Levinson, the sparks wouldn't half fly.

Me and your dad are going to the Palladium to see Viennese Nights. I wanted to go to the Scala to see Gracie Fields in Sally in our Alley but he just said we lived long enough in houses with back alleys and washing hanging out and he wants a break. Anyway it will come to the Palladium so I might get a chance later on.

I'll have to go. I can see Sadie crossing the road to our house and she has a copy of the Gazette and that's a sign she is going to talk about what shares she is thinking of buying. It's an education listening to her talking nonsense about what shares are doing well but it also gets me worked up. Sometimes I think she does it on purpose. So Tara for now. His nibs is reminding me about his PS

Your everloving

Mam

PS The Boro has been very busy, three matches in four days. Grimsby beat them 2 nil then the Boro beat Grimsby in a return match 4 nil and then the Boro lost at Ayresome Park Boro 0 Blackburn Rovers 2. And your dad says watch out for Jack Peterson, he's going to be the heavyweight champion boxer of Britain.

Saturday 9 April 1932

Dear Bob,

I did intend to write to you tomorrow but your grandma and granddad are coming for tea and I probably won't get chance. Your dad and granddad usually go to the Cleveland afterwards so unless I leave it till late on I won't have a minute on my own.

Jimmy and some of his pals were in our back arch this morning singing the football song

Camsell passed to Pease
Pease passed it back
Camsell took a rootin shot
And knocked the goalie flat
They laid him on a stretcher
They laid him on a bed
They rubbed his belly with half a clemmy
And this is what he said
Rule Britannia, two tanners make a bob
Three make eighteen pence and four two bob.

And then I heard a big argument break out and they came to me to settle it. Well not me really, Jimmy rushed in and shouted for your dad. You'd have thought your dad was at the other side of Grove Hill, instead of in Stan Cole's shed on another planet. So that's when he asked me to settle it. They were arguing was it half a clemmy or half a jelly. Well, I didn't know the answer and whatever I said I was going to make half of them unhappy so I said it all depends. All these faces were looking up at me hoping that I was going to come down on their side. So I said it all goes back to when everybody spoke Hebrew. So they said what's that. Well, I didn't know meself since I'd just made it up so I said it's what they all spoke in the bible. Well, they've heard about the bible from Sunday school so they said where in the bible so I said I couldn't remember the page but it was near the front and it was going back to when there was only Adam and Eve and when there was only one language, but when there were lots of people they spread out into different countries and started speaking different languages. So then they said where did all these people come from. The trouble with children is they always have another question when you've given your final answer. Tell them two and two make four and they say why. You were the same. I think I got the best part of my education dodging your questions. Well, I wasn't ready to give my birds and bees lecture so I said ask your Sunday school teacher, she'll know. Their Sunday school teacher is going to hate me.

Well, as I say, I had all these little faces looking up at me with puzzled expressions and I could see the wheels going round so I said when there was only one language the word was clejmellny. So they asked me to say it again and then I said later on it split into two words, clemmy and jelly. So they said when was that so I said I didn't know but they could ask their Sunday school teacher. I was beginning to like their Sunday school teacher. So it came about that the English and the Welsh say jelly and the Scots and the Irish say clemmy. So, I said, you see, you are all right. Except they weren't because our Jimmy who knows he is English had been saying clemmy was the right word when according to me he should have been saying jelly. So that was that but then I heard a big argument break out in our back arch who was the best the English and the Welsh or the Scots and the Irish. Well, as you know, we're a right ould bag of dolly mixtures round here, but they know that in the end they all have to stick together because they can't play games without each other. I thought that was the end of it but that night when your dad was in Jimmy asked him his opinion, what was right jelly or clemmy and your dad said clemmy. So then he asked him if he was English and he said yes which leaves Jimmy with a problem. I've got my fingers crossed that he doesn't come to me with it. Of course there's always his Sunday school teacher.

There are some horrible things going on here. One man has committed suicide and another at Seaham Harbour cut his wife's throat and then his own in front of their four years old daughter. Poor mite. It must have been terrifying for her. And what a thing to do anyway. But it's not only the poor who are committing suicide. The Swedish millionaire Mr Kreuger who is called the match king has killed himself although they say he was ruined financially. How somebody who is a millionaire can commit suicide because he has lost money I'll never know. How could he lose so much money? And what about his family?

I know it's no fun being poor but where there's life there's hope, as they say. You can always join Stan Cole's club and figure out how to put the world right. He was telling us that in Newfoundland near Canada one person in every five is out of work and there have been riots. They broke a picture over the Prime Minister's head and shouted throw him in the river because he wouldn't increase the dole. There was that look in Stan's eye that was saying what a good idea and the unemployed should do it here.

The Infirmary seems to be in trouble. Their income has gone down especially from the workers and the employers due to unemployment. Sir Hugh Bell and Sir Joseph Calvert who were governors have both died and I think that has something to do with it as well. There's better news from North Ormesby hospital where an extension is nearly finished and it was financed from money collected by appealing to the public. I used to work there as a ward maid cleaning the floors and that sort of thing. Now I'm Mrs Levinson's cleaning lady so my hospital training has stood me in good stead.

Mrs Levinson was telling me that a new destroyer has been launched. HMS Daring and she said it weighs one thousand four hundred tons and will travel at 36 knots. She said 36 knots an hour so for once I was able to show my superior knowledge because I remember that you told me that a knot is a speed so you don't say 36 knots an hour, you just say 36 knots. Anyway she said we are going to need it and more. There's an election in Germany going on and Hitler is being tipped to win and she says he will make war. Stan Cole says he will make war as well but Stan doesn't think that Hitler is going to come to power. The Communists will stop him.

That's all for this time. Look after yourself. We are all thinking of you and Ta Ta Pet sends his regards.

Your everloving,

Mam.

PS Boro 1 West Bromwich Albion 0 and Carnera the Italian heavyweight beat a South African on points at the Albert Hall. I don't know whose side your dad was on. I think he is happy just as long as two men are knocking seven bells out of each other.

Friday 15 April 1932

Dear Bob,

Did you know that there used to be elephants in Britain. I didn't either but elephants teeth have been discovered in Kent. Another thing they are saying is that we can't eat shell fish caught in the Tees because they are poisonous. It must be the works that are poisoning the river. Nobody else would do it. I don't know whether this includes Redcar but they are still selling winkles there.

Stan Cole got a big shock when the result of the election in Germany was announced. He was convinced that the German people would not vote for Hitler, but he travelled all round Germany, Hitler I mean, not Stan, in an aeroplane speaking at meetings all over the country and he got over thirteen million votes. Field Marshall von Hindenburg got over nineteen millions so he was elected President again. The Communist vote went down to less than four millions and they are saying that many communist voters must have switched to Hitler because of the hopelessness of the communist candidate. The French are worried because they say that Hitler is getting more and more support because there is a rising tide of nationalism and militarism in Germany being stirred up by Hitler and they are afraid of another war. Mrs Levinson says that even if Hitler was elected, and he wasn't, the business people would keep him under control because stirring up trouble to get elected is one thing but managing the economy is another and the German people will soon see through Hitler then. There are some more elections to come. I think they are to the German Parliament but I don't really understand it because we don't vote for a President and then for Parliament. We just vote for Parliament, but I suppose that between Stan, Mrs Levinson, Ta Ta Pet and your dad I will eventually get the hang of it. If he can take his nose out of his dictionary that is.

Mrs Levinson's sister from London is here for a month. Remember I told you about her. She plays the piano and got me to dance round the room while she invented a new dance, the dance of the seven dusters. I hope she wants to write another dance. I'm willing and able if she pays me like she did last time. She's a bit odd, I think. She is a great admirer of the working class. I don't know why she doesn't give her money away and join us. She could give it to me if she likes. She must have bags of it. Anyway she was playing the piano while I was round there. You can't imagine it, the sound of that piano in that big house, it's beautiful. She was playing a piece by Chopin, whoever he is, called Fantasie Impromptu. I know that because I asked her. That's what I like about Mrs Levinson and her sister, they treat me like an equal even though I'm on my knees polishing the floor and they are standing giving me orders, at least Mrs Levinson is, her sister just sits and plays the piano. She asked me if Sylvia would like a copy of the music and of course I said yes. Sylvia is getting on quite well with the piano. She is coming round tomorrow night and I will do her hair.

Stan was in last night talking about how Russia is solving the problem of unemployment with its five year plan. He said they are planning to have thousands of diesel electric locomotives and thousands of miles of new railway track, and training schools for drivers and mechanics. Mr Wells who is an engine driver here and a big union man told me that diesel electric locomotives will eventually take over from coal everywhere. This house is beginning to get like Stan Cole's shed what with Stan coming in with his socialism, Ta Ta Pet who you don't know what he is because he keeps changing depending who he is talking to and Sadie who is a right little capitalist always talking about shares. She was in last night as well and telling Stan that the shares to buy are International Tea because they paid a thirty per cent dividend last year and it is expected to be bigger this year. And she told him Home and Colonial Stores is another good one. She was just trying to get Stan going and she succeeded. He went red then purple and I thought he was going to explode so just to try to cool things down a bit I said what does thirty per cent dividend mean. But that had no effect on Stan so while he was busy going through the roof Ta Ta Pet explained to me that it means that for every one pound share the share holder would get six shillings and still have their shares. So if you had a thousand shares you would get £300. I followed Stan through the roof. It is so unfair they get all that without working. Sadie just sat there looking as if butter wouldn't melt in her mouth. She knew what she had started and now she was playing the innocent, what's all the row about. I could strangle her sometimes even though she is our best neighbour. Well, my best neighbour. Ta Ta Pet sat there looking helpful.

A Labour Councillor Mr Meehan has proposed that the means test should be abolished and he also said in the Town Hall that the ten per cent reduction in unemployment benefit should be restored. Canon Sullivan who is also a Councillor agreed with him but another Councillor said that we have to have the means test otherwise people who have money and own houses would get the public assistance as well. You can see the sense of that but it is the way that people who are poor are treated that makes it so bad. They said there are over twelve thousand out of work in Middlesbrough with over eight thousand on the means test.

The letters page in the Gazette is on the boil as well. A man signing himself Irish and proud of it wrote in about England oppressing Ireland and what with Mr de Valera wanting to separate Ireland from us has really stirred it up. England for the English has written in telling Irish and Proud of it to go back to

Ireland and Englishman has written that the Irish killed one of their finest men, Michael Collins, and he, Englishman that is, has more Irish blood in him than de Valera because his grandfather came from Dublin. There's nowt so queer as folk to quote that old Yorkshire saying. I bet they all talk with a Middlesbrough accent. Sadie's husband Paddy does because he was born in Middlesbrough although Sadie comes from Ireland.

Well, all good things come to an end and it is always a good thing for me to be writing to you. Your dad kept silent through all the row, the strong silent man as usual, but he's come to life now for his PS. So tara for now

Your loving Mam

PS There isn't a football score but your dad is unhappy with the last PS. He says its his PS and I didn't put in everything that he told me about the Carnera fight. So Carnera weighed 19 stones, the South African 13 stones 10 pounds. And Carnera has been winning on knockouts in ten rounds so to win on points must mean that he is slipping. This might be the time for your dad to get in the ring with him, sez me.

Friday 22 April 1932

Dear Bob,

Well here I am again, your ould Mam pestering you with another of her renderings. I'm not sure whether I write these letters for your benefit or my own but your dad says how much the men look forward to mail so perhaps it is for the benefit of us both.

Anyway where shall I start this week? I saw Sylvia yesterday. I went to the Co-op and she wasn't busy on her counter so we had a little chat. She said she had heard from you and will be writing back at the weekend. She was telling me that a woman in Byrneside Ave put her head in the gas oven. She was only forty two. She locked the door but when her son came home from school he saw her through the window and he shouted for help. Two men broke a window and got her out but she was in court charged with attempted suicide. She said she was tired of life and depressed. They are going to try her next Friday. It just shows how desperate it has got for some people.

Things seem strange in Germany. Hitler has an army of 400,000 brownshirts which is bigger that the German army.

The President has said that it has to be disbanded and they have agreed but they say that it has just gone underground. Hitler says that he is going to get power through peaceful means but a plot has been discovered to seize power if Hitler got more votes that von Hindenburg in the election for President. Well we know now that he didn't so we shall see what he does next. It's hard to imagine anything like that happening here. But Stan Cole says it could. What we do have is a growing army of young criminals especially in London and they are blaming unemployment for it.

Do you know the ship HMS Devonshire. According to the papers she is a county class cruiser like the one you are on and she has been sent to China to protect British residents and property. I don't know why British people want to live in China especially with all the trouble there between the Chinese and Japanese. Of course we have our own trouble here with de Valera and the Irish Government. They want a united Ireland but Mr Thomas who is the British Minister for the Dominions has said there will only be a united Ireland if that is what the people of Northern Ireland want and they don't want it, not at present anyway. And then if we look at Sweden three directors of the Kreuger match company have been arrested for fraud running into millions. No wonder people are committing suicide, even a millionaire like Mr Kreuger.

Anyway that's enough about the troubles of the world, I'm getting as bad as your dad and Stan Cole. There's an advertisement for Clubs cigarettes in the paper. It says that Jimmy Nelson the Newcastle United captain said that Dixie Dean introduced him to Clubs cigarettes and he is glad he did. Clubs cigarettes, the cigarettes with a kick in them, it says and if you save some of the packets you get a free cap. I suppose this should really be your dad's PS but I couldn't resist it. Clubs cigarettes have this effect on you.

Mr Muir was fuming the other day to Sadie. He said that in the Town Hall there was a meeting where Father Ronald Knox, I know, who's he, was speaking on Catholic Action and he said that Catholics were having larger families than Protestants and soon England will be converted to Catholicism. Mr Muir's family comes from Glasgow and there's strong feelings there. They even have football clubs that are Catholic or Protestant. So Sadie said don't look at me, we can't afford to have a lot of children, and anyway we should keep religion out of politics. I thought Stan Cole would have had something to say on the subject but he didn't, he only said that as long as they were workers they should join with Protestant workers and overthrow capitalism. I should have expected that from Stan but he always takes me by surprise, everything is so simple for him. Workers of the world unite, yet look at them in Germany fighting each other.

There's been a medium in court a Mrs Morris suing the newspapers for saying she is a fraud. It's a real laugh and I've copied it out, so here goes. "The judge was summing up when Mrs Morris suddenly closed her eyes, rose from her seat, and clutching the lapels of her costume addressed the judge in a deep voice. "Hearken to my voice, brother judge" she said. The judge said "Really we can't go on. She must sit down. We can't have all this." For a moment the voice ceased, then broke out afresh "I will say this". Someone in the court shouted "Let her speak" and the counsel for Mrs Morris said there could be harm in touching her. "Take her out" ordered the judge, but the voice besought "Do not touch her until I have left the body." The judge said it was strange that this tiny world should be receiving messages from discarnate entities in the great expanses of the universe to say that one has got a new tooth in place of another, that another's enjoying cigars and calling for more, and that another is calling for whisky and sodas.

It goes on and on and I can't copy it all out but I was lighting the fire with the Gazette that our fish and chips were wrapped in when I spotted it. I was in stitches and I thought this is too good to burn before I copy it out. So here it is.

I took it across to Sadie's and Mrs Maynard and Mrs Wilson and Mrs Henderson were in there. Honest it was a laugh a minute the things they were saying. Mrs Henderson said there's a woman in Marton Burn Rd who is a medium and she starts off with is there anybody there. She has an Indian guide called White Arrow and Mrs Henderson said Stan Cole went in and she changed the name of her Indian guide to Red Cloud. She was only joking, Mrs Henderson I mean. Stan wouldn't go near anything like that but we agreed to pull his leg and say we heard he'd been and see his reaction.

I didn't know what discarnate meant so I looked in your dad's dictionary. I'm still not allowed to touch it so I had to be careful to put it back exactly where it was so that he wouldn't know. Discarnate means stripped of flesh.

Mrs Levinson had a go at Ellen Wilkinson when I was round there. Ellen has demanded a socialist budget with the cuts in the dole and salaries to be restored. When she was asked where the money was to come from she said make it. Mrs

Levinson said that means print it and if that happened all that would then happen would be that prices would go up and we would be no better off. It makes sense, in fact they both make sense to me and that is my problem, I can't make my mind up which is right. But when you read adverts for a parlour maid fifteen shillings a week and a cook general one pound a week it does make you wonder. The bosses of the pubs are angry about the budget because it didn't reduce the tax on beer. They said it is a tax on the working man and is creating unemployment. I think they mean that if the tax was reduced by a penny a pint which is what they wanted more beer would be bought and that would make jobs. The Germans are pleased with our budget because it doesn't require them to make reparations payments to us for the war.

Well Bob, I'll have to go. There's lots more I could say but this letter is getting very long already, so tara for now. Everybody sends their regards and I have to mention Jimmy.

Your everloving

Mam.

PS Sheffield United 2 Boro 1

Friday 29 April 1932

Dear Bob,

What is Plymouth like? Can you describe it at all. How does it compare with Middlesbrough? Have you seen where Drake played bowls while the Spanish Armada was on the way to England? It all sounds very exciting to somebody like me who hasn't been outside Middlesbrough unless you count Redcar.

There's some good news from here. An order to recondition twelve whalers has been given to Smith's docks. They already have five on the slips and two just been launched to be fitted out. And the Government has put a duty on imported steel so that should help the steelworks. At least some people say it will although there are those say that all that will happen is that foreign countries will retaliate. A man who signs himself Steel Smelter has written to the Gazette and he says that British businessmen have invested in foreign steelworks to use cheap labour and the steel they produce is not as good as ours. And he says that our Chancellor of the Exchequer has calculated that we will get £5million from the thirty three and a third per cent duty on imported steel so that means that foreign steel will still be coming in. So he says that

British businessmen are putting British steelworkers out of work. It's interesting the way the arguments go. I wish I had an education so that I could argue like that. To me it's like snakes and ladders, we climb a ladder only to come down a snake when we get to the top.

We didn't go to the pictures last week so nothing to report there. The picture on at the Palladium was Shanghaied Love and I took one look at tall dark and handsome sat in the corner with his nose in his dictionary and I thought we could give Shanghaied Love a miss. So we saved some money. The people who put the pictures on are asking the Government to reduce the tax on cinema seats. They say it is a tax on the poor people's entertainment, I agree with that, and if they don't reduce the tax hundreds of cinemas will close. Which makes me think what did we do before we had picture houses. Perhaps we will have to go back to doing it whatever it was.

There's been elections in Prussia and Hitler has done well again. It's a bit complicated for me to understand but the Nazis increased their number of seat from 7 to 162 which is more than the Socialists who govern Prussia but there are other parties which help the socialists to have a majority and that includes the communists who won 57 seats. Stan Cole and Mrs Levinson agree that it is bad Hitler wining all those seats, it's about the only thing they agree on, but Stan is sure that Hitler will come unstuck if he gets enough seats to form a government. Mrs Levinson says that once he gets power he will be a dictator like Stalin in Russia. It is all very troubling but we just have to hope. But when I read that American gangsters are using corruption and threatening people so that the American congress will not end prohibition so that the gangsters can sell illegal booze at high prices it does make you wonder what the world is coming to. I don't like the way men spend their money getting drunk and Bertie Gibson wants to close the pubs here but just imagine which is the worst, what we have here or what they have in America.

Mr Walsh has just rode past with his box of pigeons on the front of his bike. He'll be off to set them off somewhere. He's a real racing pigeon enthusiast. And Mrs Smithers has just walked past with her shopping basket. She's on our side of the road so she'll be going to the bottom shops. She still comes down our end collecting the horse muck. I said to her one day I don't go down your end when a horse has done a load so why do you come down our end, and do you know what she said, she said it's a free country isn't it. What's that got to do with collecting horse muck? Anyway when the coalman's horse did a load outside our gate the other day I was there first and I saw her coming down the street with her bucket and shovel so I took my time coming in the gate to make sure she saw it was me that got there first.

Talking about low wages James Cagney the American film star has told his bosses he wants his salary increasing from one thousand dollars a week to four thousand dollars a week, and if he doesn't get it he is going back to college to continue studying for a degree. And Marlene Dietrich is at it as well though I don't know how much she wants. How's this for a joke? A Sheffield girl recently swallowed a two shilling piece belonging to her father. It is said that her father is going on as well as can be expected. That's one of Ta Ta Pet's jokes

The Prince of Wales has been up here making a plain commonsense speech in Newcastle according to the Gazette and they also said that the Prince's practical insight led him to the core of the problem. It is more a moral than an economic malady. I read it out to your dad and asked him what he thought. He just looked thoughtful as only your dad can and said he would think about it. Later on when he thought I wasn't looking I saw him reaching for his dictionary. I didn't tell him that I beat him to it. After all I'm not supposed to look in his dictionary so how could I say anything.

There've been two men hanged in Leeds side by side. I find that shocking. I know people have to pay for their crimes but to hang them side by side. One murdered his employer who was a greengrocer for forty pounds and then spent some of it on a married woman. The other murdered his landlady after a row then he walked into the police station and confessed. He is the one I feel most sorry for. What must have gone through his mind.

Joe Green the Middlesbrough boxer has his photo in the Gazette so that will please his supporters. They say he is going to be one of England's best boxers so I suppose there will be some PS's about him.

Well Bob, I must go, our Jimmy is due in from school and then it will be Mam can I have a slice of jam and bread. Everybody asks to be remembered so tara for now.

Your everloving
Mam

PS Boro 1 Everton 0 and Newcastle won the cup Newcastle 2 Arsenal 1.

Friday 6 May 1932

Dear Bob,

We've received your letter saying that you have left Plymouth and are now in Invergordon. That's the place where the mutiny started on the Norfolk last year isn't it. I hope there is not going to be any trouble this time though I don't suppose there is any reason for it now, though with the means test there is plenty of reason for it here. I've seen Dracula riding round in Grove Hill on his bike to tell some poor soul he can't really approve their application for public assistance. They've probably got something that he says they can sell before they will qualify. How I hate them. I know it's wrong to hate but I just can't help it. Your dad was on the May Day march. They started from the market in Sussex Street, marched along Linthorpe Road and down the side of Albert Park to Clairville Common carrying posters against the means test and telling the workers of the world to unite. Some hope they've got of that ever happening. They're at each others throats in Germany, and the Chinese are fighting the Japanese. And there are other countries as well.

There's a German sailing ship, the biggest in the world called the Passat, in the Tees at Billingham Wharf. She had to lower her main mast to get under the Transporter bridge.

Redcar has unveiled a tablet on Saturday commemorating the bravery of a Redcar airman called Stewart Ridley in the war. His aeroplane came down in the Libyan desert and he and his mechanic were short of water. An Australian search party found them but they were both dead. The Australians said it was obvious that Lieutenant Ridley shot himself in order to give his mechanic J Garside a chance but the mechanic died before they were found. The Australians have always mentioned them in speeches on Armistice Day and the leader of the Australian search party that found them, Captain Watts has sent a cablegram to Redcar Corporation saying "Congratulations on honouring Stewart Ridley, one of the Empire's most gallant heroes". I think that is marvelous and just imagine the Australians always remembering Stewart Ridley on Armistice Day. The tablet is at the entrance to Ridley House and it says Pro Patria. Mrs Levinson told me that means For Our Country. The tablet is on the front of the house where he was born in Coatham Road which the Corporation called Ridley House. I think that I told you that the Corporation was naming the house Ridley house in a letter some time ago. I think his family will be very proud of him, I know I would. I would be looking at that every day.

I know it is a sad reminder but on Tuesday it was two years since our Mary died. I had a little weep and gave her photo an extra polish and your dad and me went to the cemetery with some flowers. We didn't see Mr and Mrs Scrimgour but there were some fresh flowers on their little boys grave so they must have been there earlier. When we told Sylvia on Sunday that we would be going she gave us some flowers as well which was very nice of her. Your dad still takes it badly though he is improving but still goes on about the Government not spending money to find a cure for diphtheria. I think they must spend something but there is no reasoning with your dad when he gets in this mood. We all have our woes even the rich and famous. The Prime Minister is going into hospital for an operation on his eye and you know Dave Morris the comedian who was born in Middlesbrough, he collapsed on the stage at the Empire. And then you think about the number of people being killed by motor cars. What must their relatives go through when they are expecting somebody coming home and then are told by the police that they won't be coming. The Government has said that eighteen people were killed on the roads every day last year and over five hundred injured and they said that this slaughter has to stop. They didn't say how but it just shows that speed is a mixed blessing. As we won't be riding in a motor car it won't bother us but it does make you think about those who do. What goes through their minds. Your dad said nothing, everybody thinks it won't happen to them, like we thought diphtheria would never happen to us.

Well enough of the depression, life goes on and I have a responsibility for Jimmy until he is old enough to look after himself. Somebody calling himself I Enjoy One has written to the Gazette that cheaper beer is wanted in Middlesbrough not stronger beer. I wouldn't have thought it could get stronger anyway, men come from down south here thinking they can drink beer like they do down south and they end up getting a lecture in the magistrate's court about the strength of Middlesbrough beer. Anyway I Enjoy One says that it is outrageous to ask workers to pay nine pence a pint. The sooner firms put a palatable pint of beer on the counter for sixpence the better. I was standing chatting at the gate with Mrs Henderson and two other of the women in the street when Mrs Maynard came over with the Gazette and read the letter out. You know Mrs Henderson, her husband Jack comes home regularly on a Saturday night singing he belongs to Glasgow and she waits behind their front door with a frying pan to clag him, I'd like to see their frying pan, well she said if I Enjoy One really enjoys one what's he complaining about the beer is not palatable. Well you can't get round that so we said she should write a letter to the Gazette but she wouldn't. Bertie Gibson, the head lad at the Sons of Temperance came riding past on his bike and we nearly stopped him to ask him what he thought but thought better of it. Bertie on the sins of drink is not a man to cross.

There's another letter from a woman who lives in the Garden City complaining about the buses not having space for children's folding prams. Not something that bothers me I'm pleased to say. Ta Ta Pet was telling us that a friend of his was at a speech in Stockton by the Headmaster of the secondary school there. He's been to Russia and he said that people there are confident that things will get better with the five year plan. Capital punishment is abolished for thieves and murderers but people who are suspected of plotting against the government are taken out at night and murdered. I'll have to ask Stan Cole about that or get your dad to ask next time he's in Stan's shed. That's shocking. If we had that here there are streetsful of men who would disappear at night. I wonder if Mrs Levinson knows about it. I'll be in for a lecture if she does.

Well, it's time to go again Bob. Everybody asks to be remembered.

Tara for now. Write soon,

Your everloving,

Mam

PS Boro 0 Arsenal 5. So I have to tell you that there's a photo of the Boro boxer Joe Green in the Gazette. He's just beat another boxer. He won in five rounds.

Saturday 14 May 1932

Dear Bob,

I was going to write yesterday that I noticed Friday the thirteenth, not that I'm suspicious but just in case I put it off till today.

Your letter arrived and we are pleased to hear your news. Ta Ta Pet was asking about you and so I told him that you had qualified as a torpedo man and that you had been doing exercises in the Moray Firth. He said that he didn't know that cruisers carry torpedoes he thought only destroyers carried them. So I told him that was what you said and you should know. Anyway he's happy to increase his knowledge, it gives him something else to be an expert on when he's going on his rounds. Jimmy was asking what are torpedoes and your dad explained to him. So he will have something else to talk about among his pals. Middlesbrough is having a Safety Week. With 18 people being killed on the roads every day Middlesbrough Safety First Council have arranged special cinema performances at which five thousand children will be shown the Safety First Film

The President of France has been assassinated by a Russian doctor who said he was an admirer of the Italian fascist leader Mussolini and Hitler and in court he said he shot the President because the French were not intervening in Russia against the Bolsheviks. So this fascism against communism is spilling over everywhere. The papers are saying there has been a big swing to the left in the French elections. I never knew what Left and Right meant in politics until Mrs Levinson was giving me her lecture over tea and ginger biscuits. I told you that she says that ginger biscuits set the brain on fire and she obviously thinks that I need my brain setting on fire when she is giving me her lecture because we always have ginger biscuits and two cups of tea. When she is not going to give me a lecture we only have tea, usually one cup. Anyway her sister from London is still here, that's the one who used to throw bricks through shop windows to get votes for women. She was on the May Day march by the way, and they started talking about the election results in France. They were going on about the left and the right so I asked them what they meant. They said communists and socialists are left and the conservatives and fascists are right. So I said if the socialists and communists are left and the fascists and conservatives are right what are the Liberals because my father is a Liberal.

Mrs Levinson said they are on the left, and her sister said they are on the right, which left me a bit confused because they both went to university so they should know what they are talking about. I think the ginger biscuits must have been working because I said well the Liberals are in the Government and so are the Conservatives and so are Labour so what is the Government, is it left or right. Mrs Levinson said it is a national government and that not all the Labour MPs were in the government, only the sensible ones. Her sister said not all the Liberals are in either, just the stupid ones and those led by Lloyd George are outside. Mrs Levinson said that it is a national government and that is good for Britain because it is looking after the interests of everybody and Ramsay MacDonald is a hero. Her sister said that the Labour MPs like Ramsay Macdonald had sold the working class out and it is a bad government because it will not solve the country's economic problems. I think Mrs Levinson's sister would get on well with Stan Cole. And that's where it ended. The tea pot was empty and I had to go back to polishing the floor, Mrs Levinson's sister to playing the piano and Mrs Levinson disappeared into the study. I think politics is straightforward when you don't think about it. It's when you start to think about it that it becomes confusing. I wish I had gone to university so I could argue like those two but our sort don't get there. All I've got is your dad and his dictionary, and Stan Cole and Ta Ta Pet. And your grandad.

The news from America about the Lindbergh baby is terrible. The poor little thing has been found with its skull smashed in and they think it must have been killed soon after it was kidnapped. And the kidnappers demanding a ransom even when they knew the little boy was dead. There are some terrible people in the world. You wonder how they sleep at night.

And what do you think of that Mr de Valera? After all the trouble he is causing the Gazette says that most of the money for the Irish sweepstake comes from Britain and a quarter of the money over £650,000 is going to the Irish government. So the Gazette says the English are helping to pay the Irishman's taxes as well as our own. Sadie and Paddy have a share in a ticket so I asked her what she thought about it. She said she doesn't like de Valera but most of the money goes to help the Irish hospitals so it's going to a good cause. That brought my temperature down a bit.

The Americans have ordered a thousand tons of tram lines from Dorman Longs and just at the time that we are switching over from trams to buses. The Lambeth bridge in London that is being built by Dormans is nearly finished so just as one lot of work comes to an end another starts, but we need a lot more. There's an oil tanker just left Furness's shipyard to go to the Tyne for its engines and now there are no ships on the stocks so that's not good news for us. Stan Cole was on about the experience of a friend of his from North Ormesby who had to sign on at the Labour Exchange. It's no wonder it makes your blood boil. He waited for half an hour at the Labour Exchange on Monday then was told to come back tomorrow. On Tuesday he waited and then he was told to come back on Wednesday to sign on. On Wednesday he had to wait again then he signed. On Friday he waited another half an hour and signed again and was told to come next Wednesday. On the Wednesday he waited half an hour and signed again and was told to come back on Friday at 9.15am. He did and at ten o'clock he was told to come back at 11.30. He did and he stood until ten past twelve when he was told to come back at 3.30. He did and at four o'clock he was told to come back at five o'clock. He did and he stood till twenty past 6 and then he got six shillings and three pence. You can see what makes the men into rebels. The Gazette has been going on about the decline in the trade union membership. They say it is partly due to unemployment but also the unions have been becoming more political and socialist when they should stick to their earlier aims of wages and conditions of work and this has driven thousands of men away from the unions.

Some news of your old school Hugh Bell. Mr Mare who retired as the headmaster was presented with a wireless set. There's a photo in the Gazette. There's also a photo of Hugh Bell School football team and Marton Road school team who played each other at Ayresome Park in the Dorman cup final. They drew 1-1 so there will be a replay. The library just across the road from Hugh Bell has just been giver 200 books by a lady called Miss Bulmer who is a grand daughter of a mayor of Middlesbrough William Laws. I find this piece of the borough's history interesting. The library has lent out a record number of books last month. Somebody said this is a town of book lovers and music lovers and I think they were right. Well Bob, that's all this time. The jam and bread kid has just stormed in and it's Mam, can I have. So I'll have to go. He wants to be remembered to you and I have to tell you that he mentions you in his prayers every night. And of course you are in mine. Tara for now. Your everloving

Mam

PS Boro 1 Leicester City 1. This is the last match of the season. Cameron scored for Middlesbrough

Friday 20 May 1932

Dear Bob,

Just a line to tell you we are all alright and to hope that you are the same. The house is very quiet at the moment, Jimmy is at school and your dad is down at the Labour Exchange signing on. Then he is going to walk over to North Ormesby, or Doggie as people like to call it, although nobody seems to know where it got that name from. He's going to see your grannie in Alfred Street then he is calling in Testers in the market place for a hair cut and he will call in the Cuckoo on Smeaton Street to see some pals and see if there are any jobs going anywhere, then he will go to see your auntie Elsie in Coltman Street on his way home over the Longlands. We have happy memories from North Ormesby. Your dad and me were married in the Holy Trinity church in the market place and we lived with your grannie at first. Then we got that flat over the stable at the bottom of Lower High Street opposite the Bullock and Ridley's Engineering Works and Aaron Smith's coal yard. What memories this brings back. The dance hall in Lower High Street, the Pav, the Gem. Your dad always tells the tale of the local character Tea Party Tommy. This was a North Ormesby man who attended all the funerals in North Ormesby even though he didn't know the person whose funeral it was. He used to walk with all the other mourners behind the hearse and then go back to the house for the tea and cake and sandwiches. That's how he got his name.

I was telling everybody about how you told me that in the Navy when somebody dies they say he has crossed the bar. I told Ta Ta Pet as well and would you believe it, he said that there was a poem with that title written by Lord Alfred Tennyson and when he came this week he brought a copy and asked me to send you it. So here it is. I think it is a lovely poem, it has so much feeling in it.

Crossing The Bar

Sunset and evening star,
And one clear call for me!
And may there be no moaning of the bar,
When I put out to sea,

But such a tide as moving seems asleep,
Too full for sound and foam,

When that which drew from out the boundless deep
Turns again home.

Twilight and evening bell,
And after that the dark!
And may there be no sadness of farewell,
When I embark;

For though from out our bourne of Time and Place
The flood may bear me far,
I hope to see my Pilot face to face
When I have crossed the bar.

There's a poor boy of eighteen just been hanged for murdering a little girl aged six. His defence was that he was a mental defective. I wonder if they will meet their pilot face to face now they have crossed the bar in such cruel fashion. And the Lindbergh's baby that's just been cremated and those of the crew and passengers of the French liner that has just sank. The Japanese Prime Minister has just been murdered and people killed in Bombay in rioting between Moslems and Hindus. Where does it all end? It's not long since we had a war with millions killed and we don't seem to be free from more of it. I only hope something comes from the talks in Geneva. Mrs Levinson is optimistic about that.

With all these tragedies around it makes you feel ashamed to go out and enjoy yourself but just like they say, life goes on, and sitting around thinking about it isn't going to change it. So your dad and me went to the Palladium to see Edward G Robinson in Five Star Final. It's a thriller about him and Marian Marsh who owns a newspaper deciding to re-publish a murder case. The Palladium was packed and the queue stretched right round the side of the Palladium and back and then over the beck in front of the shops. We saw Sylvia there with her mother so we talked in the queue and when we came out. Sadie and Paddy were there as well.

A gang of us from Sunnyside went to Redcar on Saturday on the train seeing it was Whitsuntide. We sat the kids on the luggage racks and then we sang all the way to Redcar. It was a beautiful day and Redcar was packed and then we sang all the way back.

Stan Cole is not very pleased. Ellen Wilkinson who was our MP and lost her seat in the election has been chosen by Jarrow Labour Party to stand there. He thinks she should have stayed here. Its only last week she was in the Labour Party rooms in East Street down near the Transporter and being presented with a silver tea pot and traveling case and making a speech about the government shifting the burden from the rich to the poor. Mrs Levinson had a few words to say about it when I was round there. She doesn't have a good word for Ellen Wilkinson. But her sister stuck up for Ellen. They're a strange pair those two, you would never believe they are sisters the way they go at it about politics. Your dad said they were discussing trade with Russia in Stan's shed. He said the Russians want to buy a lot of engineering goods from us but they want credit because the food and raw materials they send us in exchange can't be sent at the same time. That seems to make sense, after all we can make things at any time but you can't grow food at any time, so they need time to pay and our Government won't give them credit. Stan says it's all political.

Mr Walsh has just rode past with his pigeons in a box on the front of his bike. He'll be setting them off somewhere to fly home. And I must fly as well before the jam and bread kid rides in. Or flies in, he's an aeroplane pilot these days so he comes in with his wings spread.

Everybody asks to be remembered,
Your everloving
Mam

PS No football score but bad news for footballers. Up till now in the close season for football the players have always got the dole but the law has been changed to make football a seasonal occupation and they are not entitled to unemployment benefit any more. Somebody in London is being paid to think up things like this. At least that's what your dad says.

Friday 27 May 1932

Dear Bob,

Your letter has arrived safely telling us you are at Invergordon in Scotland. No more mutinies I hope.

Sadie Quinn is a character. She's been over here stirring it up again talking about stocks and shares. She must have been looking out of their window to see Ta Ta Pet arrive, she knows it's his night for the insurance money, because he'd no sooner got himself settled with his book out when Sadie walked in. "I was just wanting a bit of advice" she says to Ta Ta Pet. "about some debentures I've been looking at."

Your dad looked up from his dictionary. He knows she hasn't got two brass farthings to rub together and so does Ta Ta Pet. She reads the Investors Notes in the Gazette and talks about the investments she is making. It's a kind of dream world she lives in. Your dad reckoned that Sadie only came in to ask about debentures for his benefit to get him going about capitalism. Your dad doesn't know anything about stocks and shares, he only knows about capitalism and he's against it. So he played along with it. "What are debentures?" he asked Ta Ta Pet. "They're loans to companies", said Ta Ta Pet "and the company pays interest on debentures before it pays out dividends to its shareholders".

This had your dad puzzled, and not only your dad, yours truly as well, because he couldn't see any reason for lending money to the bosses and maybe losing it if they closed their business's down like the shipyards and the steelworks are closing down. So Sadie who was wanting to air her knowledge jumped in. She said to your dad suppose you have some money in the bank and it's paying two per cent interest. What do you think you would be getting? Your dad said "Nothing". "Nothing" says Sadie, "how do make that out?" "Because I'd take it out and buy a bike" says your dad. "I'd be better off riding round the district looking for a job than sitting here looking at my bank book". "Alright" says Sadie giving up on that "let's suppose you've got nothing in the bank." "I don't need to suppose that" says your dad "I have got nothing in the bank." Sadie wasn't going to be put off by your dad being awkward. "I'm just trying to explain to you how the capitalist system works." "I know how the capitalist system works" says your dad. "Them up there" he said pointing at the ceiling "say what will happen and it does. And if they say it won't happen it doesn't as the case may be."

"Alright" says Sadie who was determined not to be beat. "Suppose I have some money in the bank, what then". "I'd ask you for the lend of a couple of bob to go to the Cleveland" he says. Instead of Sadie getting your dad worked up he was getting Sadie going. So she turned to Ta Ta Pet for a bit of intellectual support and asked him whether he thought she should buy some debentures. "Well, you've got to be careful" says Ta Ta Pet, "you don't want to risk all your legacy on one investment" and as soon as he said it he knew he had put his foot in it because he remembered she didn't have a legacy. That was something I'd made up. But it was too late to take it back. "I'm sick of hearing about my legacy" Sadie said.

"Everybody's talking about my legacy. Stan Cole has his shed, Mr Muir has his Robbie Burns, Cissy Harrison has her gramophone, Mrs Turnbull has her rhubarb wine, Mrs Rawlins has her toffee umbrellas, Mr Walsh has his pigeons, Mrs Smithers has her horse muck to put on her rhubarb, Mrs Callender has her fox fur, Sam Maynard has his rabbits, farmer Brunton's really, Mrs 'IS THERE ANYBODY THERE' in Marton Burn Rd has her Indian guide White Arrow, and I have my legacy. Except that," and she started ticking them off on her finger, "Stan Cole has his shed, Mr Muir has his Robbie Burns, Cissy Harrison has her gramophone, Mrs Turnbull has her rhubarb wine, Mrs Rawlins has her toffee umbrellas, Mr Walsh has his pigeons, Mrs Smithers has her horse muck to put on her rhubarb, Mrs Callender has her fox fur, Sam Maynard has his rabbits, though they're really farmer Brunton's, Mrs IS THERE ANYBODY THERE in Marton Burn Rd has her Indian guide White Arrow, and I don't have a legacy. I don't know who started that story that I got a legacy but I think it was Mrs Turnbull, though I can't prove it. She gets somebody in there and they have one glass of her rhubarb wine and their tongues start wagging, two glasses and their imaginations running wild, three glasses and they're away with the mixer."

I nodded my head to show Sadie I was on her side. I couldn't tell her that it was Ta Ta Pet who started it, after I told him, but I only made it up, I didn't expect him to believe me and then go and tell Mrs Turnbull. Then Sadie stormed out. I blamed your dad for getting her going although Ta Ta Pet put his foot in it as usual. She was in a right old tear with herself. And she owes me a cup of sugar. She'll be back though. Tomorrow at the latest.

There's been floods here with the heavy rain. Cambridge Rd and some houses in Jesmond Ave were flooded though there was no flooding in Grove Hill for a change. The corporation wanted to build a bigger sewer going up Green Lane but the Government told them not to as part of their economy drive. I suppose if you are down in London you don't bother about people getting their houses flooded in Middlesbrough. And those people meet in Parliament under Big Ben and I've just read that the bell for Big Ben was cast in Stockton. How about that, sitting under a clock and ignoring the people who made it. Typical.

Things might be looking up a bit here job wise. The Russians have put in a big order for steel and the boro might get some of the contract. And Dorman Long have put in a bid for a lot of work in China. Remember Joe Walton's club in Feversham Street. You went there a few times. Well they've been given some money to rebuild it. We could do with a club like that in Grove Hill but there aren't many Joe Waltons around these days.

Well, I'll have to go. It's just four o'clock so the jam and bread kid should be riding in any minute. Look after yourself. Everybody asks to be remembered.

Your everloving
Mam

PS I have to tell you that Kid Berg really won his fight with Sammy Fuller but he was cheated out of the decision. Everybody who was there thought Kid Berg had won but the referee Gunboat Smith and one of the judges voted for Fuller.

Saturday 4 June 1932

Dear Bob

Just to let you know that your letter arrived safely. You were in Scapa Flow when you wrote it. I wonder where you are now. You are certainly getting around. Anyway, just to let you know that we are all alright here's what's going on.

I went down Sunnyside looking for Jimmy last night and Mrs Callaghan was out at their gate and she got on to me about their dog Gyp. She idolises that dog and she is always talking about what it can do. So she says to Gyp "shake hands with Mrs Gill". So just to be civil I had to shake hands with it, paws really. I didn't want to. I know where my hands have been but I didn't know where Gyp's paws had been. When I got in I washed my hands straight away. Maybe Gyp washed his paws.

He's a real devil that dog, I don't know whether his mother was frightened by a bike but if anybody comes down the street on a bike he's straight at them barking at their left leg until they are out of Sunnyside. The only good thing about that is that he goes for Dracula, you know the relieving officer who goes round to make sure that people on the pancrack are not enjoying themselves. I've been told that he avoids Sunnyside if he can. Unless he is calling in Sunnyside he goes round. He'll go up Meadowfield and then along Keith Rd, or up Meadowfield and along Maple Ave, or all the way up the Vale. But sometimes he forgets and before he realises it he is in Sunnyside and Gyp is snapping at his ankle. It's quite good to watch really, Dracula pedaling with his right leg and kicking out with his left. I imagine all the curtains in Sunnyside are twitching as people are looking out and saying good dog. We call it Dracula's dance. I told Mrs Levinson's sister about it. You remember she had me dancing round the room while she invented that dance, the dance of the seven dusters and she paid me for it. So I thought if I told her about Dracula's dance it might give her an idea. I've tried to make up a dance myself. I can picture people all dressed up in fancy costumes hopping round the stage on one leg and lashing out at an imaginary dog with the other. That's as far as I get but she's the one with the imagination. I can always hop round the room while she works it out on the piano.

Sadie was back. I told you in my last letter how your dad got her mad and she stormed out but she can't stay out of our house. She can come in here and talk about stocks and shares and what she's going to buy and what she's going to sell and it's all nonsense really. But she knows it and she knows that I know it but it gives her something to keep her mind occupied. She's very intelligent really but she can't get any conversation out of Paddy and over here she can especially if Ta Ta Pet or Stan Cole is in. Any way this time she was on about buying houses. The man who writes Investors Notes in the Gazette said that buying houses is the best investment you can make. So now she's over here dreaming about buying a house. The man who writes Investors Notes said that houses built for £250 before the war are worth a lot more now and Sadie had seen one in Westwood Ave in Linthorpe advertised for sale for £575. But there's no chance of Sadie getting the money to buy a house. She hoped to win on the Irish Sweepstake but no luck. Paddy's been selling tickets and if he had sold a ticket that drew the winning horse he would have got a thousand pounds and he would have got money if he sold a ticket that drew a horse, but he didn't. We had a share in a ticket but no luck. A family in Middlesbrough called Boynton drew a horse. There was five of them and they put two shillings each in. They bought the ticket with a pen name Tommy Tittlemouse. That was the name of a horse that Mr Boynton won some money on at Catterick races so he used it to bring him luck.

Talking about money the Swedish actress in Hollywood Greta Garbo has been offered £2,500 a week to renew her contract. £2,500 a week and she's only twenty five years old, when what people are expected to live on. It's shocking. There's a letter in the Gazette from a man who says firms are paying men off when they are 65 and all they have to live on is the old age pension of ten shillings a week. I'll never understand it though Stan Cole has the answer and Mrs Levinson has the answer and your granddad has the answer and they are all different answers. The railway unions want the railways to be nationalised and the coalminers want the Government to bring back the seven hour day. Stan Cole says they should nationalise the mines as well. I think Stan would nationalise everything.

Last Sunday I went with Sadie to watch the Corpus Christi procession go by. They reckon there was 40,000 people on it. It rained which was a shame. Sadie thinks God has the answer if people would only listen. So do I but Sadie is a Catholic and we are Protestants and I sometimes wonder what God makes of it, Sadie a catholic on one side of the street and me a protestant on the other side praying to him. It must be difficult for him to sort out which are the best prayers.

Anyway to get back down to earth. Clubs cigarettes are advertising five for two pence and if you send in 150 empty packets you get a free shirt and two collars. Now that's my level. Jimmy sits the scholarship this year and I'm hoping he gets into the High School. The High School Old Boys Association has just taken over three hundred deserving boys to Redcar for the day. By deserving boys they mean boys from the poorest parts of town picked by their headmasters. They say that some of these boys have never seen the sea. I can't understand that at all. The sea is only walking distance from Middlesbrough. The boys round here walk along the black path to the breakwater and to Redcar. A bottle of water and a jam sandwich, that's me when I'm talking posh, like when I go to Mrs Levinson's, but samwidge when I'm talking Middlesbrough. They walk to Eston and Roseberry Topping and all over the place and think nothing of it.

There's more trouble in Germany. They have a Chancellor like we have a prime minister, and he's just resigned because he wanted to give some of the big landowners land to the poor and the President wouldn't let him. Hitler wants his job because the Nazis are the biggest party in their Parliament but people are worried about what he will do if he gets power. So the German President Hindenburg won't give him the job. The German President is something like our king except he is elected. Well, we'll see what happens. That's all for this time. Everybody asks to be remembered.
Tara for now,

Your everloving,
Mam.
PS. No football yet so I have to tell you that Larry Gains the British heavyweight boxer beat Carnera over ten rounds on points. The boxing experts here, outside the ring that is, say that Carnera made the mistake of trying to box Larry Gains and that's why he lost. He should have gone for a knockout. What Larry Gains would have been doing in the meantime they don't explain. It's all so easy when you're just an expert outside the ring. Oh, I forgot, Mrs Smithers beat me to the horse muck again, right outside our front gate. I don't know how she does it.

Friday 10 June 1932

Dear Bob,

How are you? Here I am sitting looking out the window for inspiration. Yagbo bottles or jars hurry up now has just gone past. He's offering paper windmills for old clothes. Charlie McMann the ice cream man has just gone by as well and the coalman. It's a really busy day in Sunnyside. That's two horses and a handcart in the space of an hour. I went out with my bucket and shovel just in case but nothing. If I hadn't gone out there would have been a load of horse muck and Mrs Smithers would have been there with her bucket and shovel. No sign of her. It's uncanny the way she knows. It's getting so bad I can hardly bring myself to speak to her but you have to be polite. She always speaks to me but when she does she has a smile on her face with a sort of a look of triumph about it. After all I never go up her end yet she always comes down ours. Your dad thinks it's a great joke and tells me not to get my bowels in an uproar but it's alright him talking, it's for his garden. Well ours really. He does all the work and leaves me to collect the horse muck.

He's got his nose stuck in that dictionary of his so it's all quiet from that corner at the moment but just wait till he thinks I'm getting to the end of this letter and he'll be telling me about his PS. East of Borneo was on the Palladium. The Gazette said it was a daring drama of the Malay jungle but it's all drama in this house and I wanted something to laugh at for a change so we went to the Gaumont to see Laurel and Hardy in Beau Chumps. Did you know that Stan Laurel was born in North Shields? Him and Oliver Hardy are coming to England for a holiday. I don't know how much they get paid but Greta Garbo is going to be paid three thousands pounds a week. Just imagine that if you can. We'd be grateful for three.

Sadie's been in talking about her dealings in shares. She's as bad as some of the fellas round here with the horses. They talk about nothing else. They study the papers and form books and talk about the owners and the jockeys and the races the horses won in the past and the handicap and on the flat and over the sticks and the odds. It's their life and stocks and shares seem to have become Sadie's. It's gambling just the same but Sadie says yes but you get your money back with stocks and shares, except she doesn't have any money to spend on it. With her it's all in the imagination She's becoming really expert though about the types of shares and which ones to buy, but that's where it ends. She's even got a book out of the library about it.

We have a good library in Middlesbrough. The children's librarian Miss Halbert has won the Scottish Libraries Association essay competition and has gone on a tour of the libraries in London. So that's something else we have to be proud of in Middlesbrough. Ta Ta Pet said Cyril Smith who plays the piano has been on television in London. I'd never heard of television but it's something like the wireless only they send pictures instead of sound according to Ta Ta Pet.

. Maybe one day Sylvia will play like Cyril Smith, she's putting plenty of practice in. Middlesbrough is going to have a film made about the steel industry here. It's called Men of Steel and it's being made at the Acklam steelworks. So fame at last. And what do you know, we are now selling slag from the steelworks. The demand for steel is down and the demand for slag is up. What a strange world we live in. There's work for a hundred men. Your dad went down to the Ayresome wharf where a Mr Cruddas has a slag crusher and a ship to carry the slag for road building to London. Your dad was too late to get taken on, and anyway he doesn't really want a job as a labourer, but it would have been better than nothing.

I've been reading that the Navy is trying to salvage the submarine that sank, the M2. She is lying in a hundred feet of water. Divers have cut holes in her hull and fitted air hoses but I can't see what good pumping air in now would be. The men are long dead. Which reminds me have you heard about the ghost ship? It's a wooden ship with no crew on it and they reckon it has been at sea for a hundred years. How they can tell that when they don't even know its name I don't know.

Perhaps there are things on it that people were using a hundred years ago.

A little girl here only two years and ten months has pulled a pan of boiling water over herself and died in North Ormesby hospital, poor little thing. I can't imagine what her parents were doing to leave a pan of boiling water where a bairn could pull it over. They must be going through a terrible time now.

There's a big argument been going on in the letters in the Gazette about a bird that somebody heard singing at Normanby. Some say it was a nightingale and others say it was a blackcap and it's getting a bit hilarious because somebody is poking fun at the letter writers. He says it must be a nightingale because only a nightingale would be encouraged to sing by throwing a stone at it. Blackcaps would fly away. You wonder how they think them up.

Stan Cole walked in the other night while Sadie was here and he started to get Sadie going by asking her what she thought of de Valera. The Prime Minister Ramsay McDonald has gone to Dublin to try to talk de Valera out of breaking links with Britain. It turned into a right old shindig because Sadie doesn't like de Valera so when Stan said she was Irish so she must be a supporter of de Valera Sadie said she wasn't a nationalist she was working class. That gave Stan his chance because he said, working class and dealing in stocks and shares. Sadie can take a lot of ribbing and she can dish it out as well but this was a bit below the belt because Stan knows that Sadie studies stocks and shares but doesn't have the money to buy them. So Sadie flew off the handle and told Stan what she thought of him and his politics. It was quite an education watching the pair of them but eventually Stan said he was only pulling her leg and it all got smoothed down. But Sadie had the last word because she told him some shares to buy to make a profit. That got Stan worked up but he had no answer, at least not one that he could think of immediately because as soon as he opened his mouth Sadie reminded him that Mrs Dorman has just given one thousand pounds to the Nunthorpe parish church in memory of her husband so the capitalists can't be all bad.

Talking about a strange world and film stars Hollywood is making a film about the Arctic and they have taken snow to the Arctic. It's made out of bleached corn flakes and feathers and they have taken a wind machine with them. I didn't know there was such a thing as a wind machine apart from the ones I have to listen to round here.

Well Bob, I must go. Your dad has gone out and forgotten to give me his PS. I think he is in Stan Cole's shed sorting out the world's problems. So Tara for now,
Your everloving,
Mam

Friday 17 June 1932

Dear Bob,

How are you, well I hope. We received your card from Lamlash. The Isle of Arran seems very romantic. Your dad worked in the shipyard at Ardrossan which is where you get the ferry to Brodick which your dad said is on Arran. When we have some money I would like to go to Scotland.

The other day Mrs Maynard and Mrs Muir were talking just outside our gate. I was looking out the window trying to make out what they were talking about but I couldn't hear a word and I couldn't read their lips. Then I remembered that our front bedroom window was open, it was such a fine day so I went upstairs and they were talking about Dracula the relieving officer and how he had refused somebody in Hollyhurst any assistance. He's a horrible man. Anyway, if you remember I told you about how Gyp always runs after him when he comes through Sunnyside on his bike and barks and snaps at his ankles and how Dracula kicks out at Gyp and how I had invented a dance called Dracula's dance where the dancers hop round the stage on one leg kicking out with the other. Well, listening to those two talking about him reminded me so I thought I would have a rehearsal. So I went downstairs and stood thinking about it and how it would go. I think you have to put yourself into the situation if you are going to get it right so I imagined it was me riding the bike with Gyp barking and snapping at me. Well, I don't have any trousers like Dracula but I thought I would put your dad's bicycle clips on anyway just to get the atmosphere right. Well I was hopping round with your dad's bicycle clips on kicking out with my left leg and I kicked the table leg. It was really painful. I was limping round for hours. It was so painful I forgot to take your dad's bike clips off and he walked in for his dinner. What you doing with my bicycle clips on he sez. Well I couldn't explain to him about Dracula's dance, you know what your dad's like, so I said I was cleaning up in the back kitchen and accidentally knocked his clips off the nail where they hang. Well he said they don't hang on a nail in the back kitchen they're kept in the drawer. Your dad can be really awkward sometimes. So I said yes I know but I was cleaning the drawer out and I picked the clips up and forgot to put them down and I still had them in my hand when I walked into the back kitchen and to save time I just hung them up on the nail. So he said well if they were hanging up on the nail how do they come to be on your legs. So I had to explain to him, your dad's a bit slow on the uptake, that when they fell off the nail to save time hanging them up again I put them on my legs and then the next time I walked into the front kitchen I would take them off and put them back in the drawer which is what I was going to do when you walked in.. He just shook his head, you know the way he does, and said where's me dinner.

Then our Jimmy came in for his dinner and asked me why I was limping so I said I hurt my leg playing football. So he sat down and had his dinner, we were having corn beef stew with suet puddings done in the oven. Then after he had finished his dinner he asked me who I was playing football with. Honest, our Jimmy asks some gormless questions sometimes. He thinks I am just an old woman who gives him jam and bread and a clip now and then to keep him on the straight and narrow. He's a big lad like your dad and he's good looking like your dad but he's got brains like your dad. He doesn't take after my side of the family at all.

The news from America about the Lindbergh baby is shocking. Mr and Mrs Lindbergh paid ten thousand dollars ransom money and the kidnappers knew the baby was dead. A maid who worked for Mr Lindbergh's mother was questioned three times and when she knew they were going to question her again she committed suicide. She was English and the Lindberghs don't think she had anything to do with it. Anyway they are going to make kidnapping a federal offence punishable by death.

Ta Ta Pet was in and full of information as per usual. He said that Greta Garbo is getting three thousand pounds a week to make her next film and that's one thousand three hundred pounds a week more than she was getting before. He said that she had lost all her money in the Kreuger crash, remember I told you about the Swedish match millionaire whose firm went bust.

When I was round at Mrs Levinson's house she was talking about Greta Garbo. She said her sister in London who produces things for the stage knows Greta Garbo and was saying that she lost her money when the First National Bank in California failed and closed its doors. I said Ta Ta Pet told me that she had invested her money in Mr Kreuger's match company and that's where she lost it. My dear, says Mrs Levinson. Now when Mrs Levinson calls me her dear I know that's the start of one of her lectures. I don't mind, it's better than washing floors and I'm learning all the time except Stan Cole undoes it. My dear, she said, the bank failed. So I said how can a bank fail. So she said My dear you know when you put money in the bank. That was a tricky question for me because I have never put money in a bank. I've never been inside a bank so I didn't know what to say. If I said yes it would mean that I have money in the bank and Mrs Levinson would think I am well off and maybe she wouldn't pay me so much. If I said no it would seem impolite so I didn't know what to say. So I had a fit of coughing which went on a bit and she didn't know whether I said yes or no. Then she said with a cough like that I better have a drink so she told me to make the tea and bring the ginger biscuits. Then while we were drinking the tea she started on her lecture again. How do you think banks make a profit she asked me. I had no idea and I felt it was safe to say so. When you put money in the bank she said the bank invests most of it and they keep some in the bank just in case you want to draw some out. Now if the bank over invests or it makes bad investments like lending it to a company like Kreuger who goes bankrupt and the customers who have put their money in the bank all decide to draw their money out at the same time the bank can't repay them So the bank fails and it shuts its doors. Do you understand she asked. I nodded like I'd been nodding all the time while I was eating my ginger biscuits. And there's one thing I knew for sure and that was if I ever have any money I'm not going to put it in a bank

Talking about banks Sadie was in and she was talking about buying some shares in the International Tea Company because they are paying a 30% dividend. Sylvia was in at the time and she doesn't know about Sadie's wild dreams of getting rich without working. Sylvia had been to a meeting at which Mrs Schofield Coates was in charge and there was an Indian woman speaking and she said that the average income in India is two pence a day which means that some people get less. Sylvia was really indignant. How could Sadie talk about buying shares in the Tea Company when people in India were getting wages like that. And India is governed by us, it is part of our Empire and people are not allowed to hold meetings and are sent to prison and can be flogged. She went on and on. You would have thought it was Stan Cole on his soap box. Poor old Sylvia was really getting her bowels in an uproar and we had to calm her down. Sadie said she was not going to buy shares, she was only saying that to expose the capitalist system. She wasn't really, who knows what goes on in Sadie's mind. It's all a sort of game she plays, but she is learning things by doing it and teaching me as well.

Did I tell you that a film is being made at Dorman Long's Acklam works called Men of Steel. There's a photo in the Gazette of some of the actors on Middlesbrough station. They are staying at the Corporation Hotel. Your dad had a pint there once in the bar at the back not in the posh part. Two of the actors were dressed up as steelworkers and the actress was dressed up to work in the office. Some of the men who work there are extras in the film.

Well Bob, I better go. This letter seems rather long but there is so much happening and any minute now the jam and bread kid will come riding in. Everybody asks to be remembered, so Tara for now.

Your everloving,
Mam

Friday 24 June 1932

Dear Bob,

How are you? We have received your card from Llandudno in Wales. It's right what they say, join the Navy and see the world although I never expected you would go to Wales. There are a lot of Welsh people living in Middlesbrough with a Welsh church in Southfield Road, a Welsh choir and we even have an Eisteddfod. They came here to work in the steel industry. Now a lot of them are unemployed. Talking about churches there has been a Methodist conference going on here for over a week. I didn't know there are three kinds of Methodists and they have been holding a conference in Middlesbrough to talk about uniting. There are united Methodists, Wesleyans and Primitive Methodists. Guess where there are lots of primitives. I don't know what it means but they started off in Stockton in 1831 and spread to Middlesbrough. When they all join together there will be 24 churches in Middlesbrough. Eleven Wesleyan, seven Primitive Methodists and six United Methodists. Sylvia was telling me all about it. She's a

Wesleyan and she's been going to the conference when she could. She went on their march along Linthorpe Rd to the High School playing field. There were three thousand of them. And they had a mass choir in the Town Hall with people from Stockton, Middlesbrough and South Bank. I think I'll join the Wesleyans and I could go to church with Sylvia and her mother. They seem to talk a lot of sense. They've been condemning lots of things, Sunday cinema, indecency in films, drink and gambling, capitalism. They even said that buying shares is gambling, and they really went to town on the means test. They sound a lot like Stan Cole except Stan likes a drink and he doesn't believe in God, at least he says he doesn't. Whereas they say that if we followed the laws of God and the ways of Jesus there would be no wars. And they even say that tariffs on trade are wrong because the people of the world should be united.

Bertie Gibson was very pleased with the conference because it praised the temperance societies, Mr Gibson is their head lad round here, for commemorating the 100th anniversary of the signing of the pledge by the Seven Men of Preston. So you can tell all those men on your ship who don't take their rum about the Seven Men. I bet they never knew they existed. And in America prohibition is going to be the big issue in the election for President. President Hoover's Republican Party will let each state decide if it wants to continue to prohibit the sale of alcohol. The gangsters are in favour of prohibition so we know which way they'll be voting.

Talking about South Bank there's a letter in the Gazette from a man calling himself Uncle Mac of the Wild Goose Association of Slaggy Island. He's having a go at some of the people who have been writing in about whether a bird at Normanby was a nightingale or a black cap. I told you about it. Anyway this is what Uncle Mac wrote. "I regret to note your correspondent Entomolist doubts the existence of the Wild Goose Association of Slaggy Island and also the authenticity of the author Hyam Moulting. It pains me very much that any student of bird life does not know of this wonderful organisation and its famous books of reference." I wish I could write witty letters like that. When I read these letters I wonder which school they went to. I went to Archibald school till I was fourteen and your dad went to Lawson but he had to leave when he was thirteen to get a job. He's making up for it with that dictionary of his.

Sadie came in while Sylvia was here and started on about shares again. Sylvia knows now that she is only talking about it so she didn't get upset when she started on about shares in Corry and sons who sell coal and oil having a dividend of seventeen and a half percent. But she did say that it was immoral because the miners get such low wages and the owners of the mines are trying to make them work longer hours. So then they got into a discussion about shares. Sylvia said that buying shares is gambling but Sadie knows that.

Dorman Longs have got a contract for two bridges in China so that means some work here. A bridge over the River Thames in Lambeth in London was opened last week by the King. That's another Middlesbrough bridge but I bet nobody said anything about that. Just think of all the people who will cross that bridge, like in Australia, and if you mentioned Middlesbrough to them they'd say, Middlesbrough, where's that not knowing that they were actually standing on a piece of our town. I get angry when I think of it, what the people of Middlesbrough have done and could do yet they are talking of giving work to men on outdoor relief by building a flood prevention scheme in Linthorpe. Ta Ta Pet was saying that in Seattle in America there are fifty thousand people out of work and they have formed an association where the members work for two days a week and get food and clothes in return. They don't use money. When I said that sounds good he said that it won't work because it is going back to barter when there was no money and people just exchanged things. He did go into it but it is too long winded to tell you about it here but what he said made sense. I told you he goes to night classes and he is reading about economics so that he can get promotion.

Honest, the more you look into things the more they seem to be different to what you thought. Our Government is attending talks in Geneva about disarmament and then I read that we are exporting arms worth nearly three and a half million pounds which is nearly a third of all arms exported in the world. There's a conference of Labour Party women in Brighton who want to stop arms being exported to Japan and any country which is threatening to attack Russia. Mrs Levinson says that making arms provides work and if we didn't do it all those men and women would be out of work and somebody else would be making the guns. Think your way out of that one. I told Stan Cole what Mrs Levinson said and he said the workers of the world should unite and refuse to fight.

So I said what about in the meantime and he just repeated what he had said.

I told you about Sadie having Mr Muir on about the Scots Burns night in the Town Hall. Well he got one back the other day. Sadie and me were talking at her gate when Mr Muir came along. He said I see you lot in Ireland are ruled by a Red Indian. Sadie asked him what he was talking about and he said that an Indian Chief of the Chippewayan tribe is attending a conference in Dublin, and Mr de Valera was made a chief of the tribe some years ago. He is known as Eagle Dressing His Feathers. Mr Muir was in stitches and he went on down the street chortling away and I think Sadie was shell shocked. She couldn't get over it. She kept saying eagle dressing his feathers. I'd like to be in their house when Paddy comes in.
Well Bob, that's all for this time. I can hear the tramp of tiny feet coming in the back door and any minute now it will be Mam can I have a slice of jam and bread. So Tara for now.
Your everloving,
Mam

Friday 1 July 1932

Dear Bob,

I hope that you are well. The last we heard from you you were in Llandudno. We are wondering where you are now. Don't forget to send us a post card. I am saving all the post cards you send so that at some time in the future we can look at them and see where you have been. Also we can look these places up in the Atlas and Jimmy will learn a bit about geography.

We had an awful thunderstorm here the other night. It kept me awake, I've never heard thunder like it and the rain came down in buckets. Your dad slept through it of course.

Mr Walsh has just gone past on his bike with his pigeons in a box on the front. He spends an awful lot of time with those pigeons and on his allotment. Mrs Walsh doesn't mind, she says it takes him out of the house. He had some pigeons in a big race last week. He had to send them by train. He didn't win anything. I sometimes wonder how he can afford it but he grows a lot of things on his allotment and in his garden. He's a keen gardener, one of the best round here, and that is saying something. Your dad spends his time in Stan Cole's shed putting the world right. At least Mrs Walsh can see something for what Mr Walsh does. Your dad was out last night with Mr Maynard and his nets on farmer Brunton's farm. My heart's in my mouth all the time they are out. I saw Mrs Masterman the policeman's wife at the Maynards with her shopping bag. Mr Masterman knows everything that goes on round here. Ta Ta Pet was saying that giving the local bobby a rabbit is nothing, in Chicago the police are paid by the gangsters who run the speakeasies. That's because the city is bankrupt through rotten politics and the police have not been paid for three months. I couldn't believe it but he had cut it out of a paper and he showed me it and there it was in black and white.

Well, what's going on in the town. There's a new Jewish cemetery been opened, there's a letter in the Gazette from somebody who says that vandals are proposing to turn Victoria Park, that's the little park in front of the Town Hall into a car park, and Dorman Long have got a contract to build a bridge in Denmark. How's that for a quick report on what's happening in the boro. The people who live at Nunthorpe are up in arms about developers wanting to build more houses there. Speculators have bought land to lay sewage systems for houses along Gypsy Lane, Gunnergate Lane and Dixon's Bank and the residents are saying Nunthorpe will be joined on to Middlesbrough instead of being a village. I think they are right, we don't want the villages to be joined to Middlesbrough, there will be no countryside left and that is what makes Middlesbrough such a nice place. We are near the sea, we are near the country and we are near the hills. The kids can walk to all these places. Your dad and me used to. Now all he thinks and talks about is politics. I just hope it stays at talking. In Germany the Nazis and the communists are killing each other and these are ordinary working men that we are talking about. They've gone crazy. And in Italy two anarchists, whatever they are, have just been shot for trying to assassinate Mussolini. I'm glad it is not like that here though Mrs Levinson says the revolutionaries will bring it here if they have their way.

Jimmy's school, Marton Grove is in the Gazette. There's a photo of their athletic team and the headmaster Pop Morgan. Well the kids call him Pop, but we call him Mister. You have to have respect for teachers. The boys have won all kinds of events and the relay team won the Gazette shield. Talking about teachers how's this for a bit of a laugh. The Town Council has agreed to increase the pay for part time lecturers at Constantine College to nine shillings an hour. Some councillors were against the increase and the deputy mayor told a story about a specialist who once charged five guineas for tapping a wheel with a hammer. And he said that he charged five shillings for hitting the wheel and five pounds for knowing where to hit it. The deputy mayor said these lecturers are specialists and we have to maintain the standard of education in the town. You can't disagree with that. At least I can't. I want our Jimmy to get a good education like that. Talking about railways the LNER is cutting down on the maintainence of the railway lines. That means they will need less rails from Dormans which will mean more men out of work. It's just one thing after another. The works are closed down so there is less traffic on the railways so they cut down and there's less work for the steel works. And so it goes on. They are even closing their locomotive works at Gateshead. Three miners have met an awful death in Felton colliery. I'm not sure whether that is in Durham or Northumberland, but the cage they were in fell to the bottom of the shaft which was flooded and they were drowned. That is shocking. How could a cage fall to the bottom of the pit shaft? Somebody hasn't done their work properly. There's always somebody getting killed at work. The Gazette says 28 men were killed in Middlesbrough works last year. You have to live through this to understand how women feel. I'm glad you are not in the works and if I have my way Jimmy will not go there either.

A man in India has a letter in the Gazette saying that in a village near where he is living Indian boys are wearing a medal with Middlesbrough coat of arms on one side and on the other it says HWF Bolckow first Member of Parliament for Middlesbrough. The man says that he was told by the boys that a sahib had distributed the medals as buckshish. I wonder if that is where we get the word bukshee from meaning it costs nothing.

There was four of us women standing at our gate yesterday afternoon talking. Your dad calls it gossiping. Men talk, women gossip. When he says that, I say that the king is a man, the Prime Minister is a man and all the government are men and look at the state the country is in with them doing all the talking. But he doesn't take any notice. Anyway we women were standing there gassing, your dad was down the garden burning some garden rubbish, when along came Mr Muir. He hasn't forgotten the time Sadie and me had him on about him being in the Gazette in his kilt and dickie bow at the Burns' supper. Anyway he said good afternoon then he stopped and started looking up at the sky. We all wondered what he was looking at and after a bit we all started looking. And he just stood there looking without saying anything so eventually I said what you looking at. He said he was just looking at the smoke signals in the sky. Well, it was the smoke off your dad's bonfire coming over the roof. Mr Muir said it was smoke signals from Eagle Dressing His Feathers in Dublin to the Irish in Middlesbrough and he asked Sadie if she could read it for him So she said yes she could, it read could Jock Muir lend Paddy Quinn a couple of bob to get in the Cleveland tonight. Well we all burst out laughing and poor old Jock went on his way muttering I don't know what. Well, that's all I have to say this time. Your dad and me went to the Gaumont to see Frankenstein. Boris Karloff was the monster which makes a change from Ramsay MacDonald. Everybody asks to be remembered so tara for now

Your everloving, Mam

PS Your dad says I have to tell you about that American boxing referee Gunboat Smith. He's done it again. In the Jack Sharkey Max Schmeling fight the crowd thought that Schmeling won. He's a German. But Gunboat Smith and one judge said Sharkey won on points. Everybody round here is saying that you can't win in America, the referees see to that. It can't be such a great place. The paper says that twenty thousand people committed suicide there last year and there were twelve thousand murders. That's a lot of unhappiness in God's own country.

Friday 8 July 1932

Dear Bob,

How are you? I have to ask you that just to be polite and anyway I have to start somewhere and it's as good as talking about the weather. That's the perennial subject in England. Mrs Levinson told me that the reason people never say good day to each other when they meet in the street in a morning is because they don't know what it's going to be like in the afternoon. I didn't know that but it makes sense. I told it to Ta Ta Pet and he didn't know either but once he gets a glass of Mrs Turnbull's rhubarb wine inside him it will be round Grove Hill before you can say Jack Robinson.

I wonder where that saying came from, Jack Robinson. Why Jack Robinson? I was lying in bed the other night thinking about that and I couldn't think of a reason so I gave your dad a dig and asked him but he just said he will take it up in Stan Cole's shed tomorrow. So I lay there thinking maybe he was a highwayman or a riveter like your dad. I mean a riveter like your dad, not a highwayman. But if he was a riveter why Jack Robinson. Joe Gill is a lot shorter. I think I'll start saying that and maybe it will catch on and we'll be famous. On the other hand the police might start saying who's this Joe Gill we keep hearing about, we better investigate and with your dad sometimes going out with Sam Maynard catching rabbits that would not be a good idea. I think I'll stick with Jack Robinson.

Just to keep you up with the history of Middlesbrough I have to tell you that Mrs Suffel one of the boro's oldest citizens has died aged 76. His nibs wants you to know that because she is or was an important part of the history of the town. I'll bet she had a lot of interesting stories to tell. It's a pity they are not written down. She was the wife of Robert Boyd the England and International sculling champion. That should warm the cockles of your sailor's heart. He was also the boss of the Shakespeare at yon end of Linthorpe Road although I don't suppose you need me to tell you where that is. I know your dad has taken you round some of the pubs down the town. Anyway, her father was called Bell and he was the boss of the Alexandra in Hill Street. That's where they met and they eloped to Gateshead and got married in a registry office. He was a Geordie but came to live in Middlesbrough after they got married. After he died, and they were only married seven years, she was the boss of the Shakespeare for a lot of years so she was well known. She got married again to a man called Boyd. Your dad says the Shakespeare kept the best pint of Bass in the town, and he should know. That was when he was single living in North Ormesby but now we live in Grove Hill he doesn't get down the town much. He tries to pass the Cleveland but I think an invisible hand comes out and drags him in. Either that or something trips him up and he falls in.

By the way talking about sculling and cockles I told Ta Ta Pet what sailors mean when they are out rowing and they say they caught a crab, meaning that one of their oars has got stuck in the water down the side of the boat. That's something else he didn't know. I'm glad I do. I would feel an awful fool if I was talking to a sailor and I said you had caught a crab when you were out rowing and I thought it meant you caught a real crab. My education is really improving.

There's an awful story in the papers. It is something that happened a bit ago but it was in the paper wrapped round our fish and chips. I get a good read sometimes like that. Anyway this is about an officer in the Army Captain Blackley. He was married but fell in love with another young girl so he didn't let on that he was already married and she married him. But he knew that he had committed bigamy and had decided before they were married that he would commit suicide after the honeymoon and because he said he thought that she wouldn't want to live without him he shot her as well. He wrote a note to the coroner saying "I know she would die if I told her and so I am taking her with me. I feel sure she will be waiting for me when I turn the revolver on myself." Mrs Levinson was livid about it. She called him cruel and arrogant and said officers don't act like that and she said that if there is any justice in this world that girl will be waiting for him alright but not in the way he thinks. I also read that a sailor got six strokes of the cat and eight months hard labour for assaulting a woman and stealing her handbag. I am telling you about this because I want both my sons to treat girls as human beings and as equals not playthings. Here endeth the lesson.

Mrs Levinson was also on about votes for women in France. The things she said that French senators said when a bill to give the vote to women was introduced in their Senate which is the same as our Parliament, I think, about votes for women. One of then said Frenchwomen don't want the vote. Mind you when I see what goes on here I can tell them they are in for a shock when they get it. Another man said that when his wife gets the vote he won't vote. And he said that countries like Britain, Germany and America where women have the vote also have the worst economic crisis. Mrs Levinson was really on her high horse about it, she felt so bad about it she even got the ginger biscuits out and gave me one of her lectures. I think I told you that her sister who lives in London used to throw bricks through shop windows to get the vote for women. I suppose it runs in the family.

I just don't understand what is going on in America or in the world. In Philadelphia I read that the Committee for Unemployment Relief say that they have run out of money and two hundred thousand people face starvation. In Chicago policemen get forty five dollars a week that's £9 and they haven't been paid for three months. There are over twelve thousand speakeasies run by gangsters in Chicago and they are paying the policemen's' wages. Stan Cole knows what's wrong. Capitalism. Mrs Levinson knows what's wrong. The Americans have prohibition and they don't have our historic traditions. I know what prohibition means but not what our historic traditions means but I didn't want to say so in case there would be a long explanation and I had a lot of work to do before I could go home. Sadie was in talking about shares again. She's been advised to buy shares in Dunlop Rubber, Imperial Tobacco, International Tea and Cunard Shipping. I don't know who her advisor is but he obviously doesn't know that Sadie hasn't got two halfpennies to rub together. I don't think she has an advisor really, she's just making it up.

Mrs Levinson said the King is going to inspect the fleet in Weymouth on 11 July and HMS Norfolk will be there. She showed me it in The Times. I feel like I have to curtsey when she shows me The Times. She seems to say it in capital letters. Mr Levinson reads the stocks and shares in The Times every morning before he goes to work. Anyway it says there will be sixty warships in Weymouth, battleships, cruisers, aircraft carriers, submarines. And the names are there and I felt so excited when I saw HMS Norfolk. You will write and tell us all about it won't you?

Well I will have to go now, tea time approaches and that means the jam and bread kid. And it will soon be chucking out time at Stan Cole's shed. Everybody asks to be remembered. Look after yourself.

Your everloving, Mam

PS There's been a smash and grab raid at Collingwood jewellers on Linthorpe Rd. It's getting like America. And your dad said I have to tell you that Len Harvey was beat on points for the world middleweight title by the Frenchman Marcel Thil. I think that's the spelling.

Friday 15 July 1932

Dear Bob,

How are you? Well I hope. We've received two cards from you, one saying you are in the Scilly Isles and the other that you are in Weymouth. That would be for the King to inspect the fleet. I hope you are going to tell me all about it and what you had to do on your ship. Jimmy wants to know why they are called Scilly Isles which he thinks is silly isles. I don't know and your dad doesn't know but he said he will ask in Stan Cole's shed.

There was blood on the moon here the other day. Mrs Rawlins had made a trifle, you know sponge cake at the bottom and jelly and custard on the top, and because it was hot she put it out on the window sill to catch the breeze and help it to set. Anyway the kids were playing tip tap in the street, you remember the game, you put a bit of wood sharpened at both ends on the ground and hit it with a stick and when it bounces up into the air try to whack it with the stick. Well, the boy that was in whacked it alright and the bit of wood landed in the middle of Mrs Rawlins trifle. The kids all scattered of course and Mrs Rawlins didn't know anything about it until she went to bring the trifle in and there was this bit of wood sticking up out of it. You should have heard her. She was going to strangle whoever did it when she caught the culprit and she was going to ask God for his help in catching him. Sadie asked Ta Ta Pet if Mrs Smith could claim on her insurance for it but Ta Ta Pet said the insurance company would say it was an act of God and anyway she only had a penny a week on her husband and that wouldn't cover the trifle. But I don't think Mrs Rawlins would throw the trifle away. She would just pull the bit of wood out and if there was any muck she would just scrape it out. You can't throw a good trifle away just for that.

Jimmy was asking me why the prairie would echo in the song he's been learning at school God Bless the Prince of Wales. Well I don't know the song, your dad doesn't and the folks I asked round here don't know it. As it seemed important to Jimmy and he didn't dare ask his teacher I mentioned it to Ta Ta Pet. He knew it. He was taught it and he said it was written by a man called George Linley. But he didn't remember anything about the prairie echoing so I told Jimmy to sing it. It turned out that it wasn't God let the prairie echo it was God let the prayer re-echo. Trust Jimmy to get it wrong. He just stands there with his solemn eyes. You know I look at our Jimmy and I see a bit of your dad in him. Well a lot really. I suppose there might be a bit of me in there somewhere lurking in the bushes. We'll have to hope one day it will come out.

There's uproar between the Labour Party here and the Unemployed Association. The Labour Party have an open air meeting every week in Newport Crescent, that's down the town off Linthorpe Rd. and the speaker Mr Cocks who is the Labour Party's agent kept getting heckled. He said that a demonstration of unemployed outside the Town Hall last night that the police had to control was organised by the Middlesbrough Unemployed Association not the Labour Party. The Labour Party are saying that the Unemployed Association is run by communists and the Labour Party has nothing to do with it. Stan Cole says that it isn't but I'm not sure that I would believe Stan about that but anyway why aren't the Labour Party organising people to demonstrate against unemployment. Not that I think it will do much good but at least it would show that they cared.

There was a deputation from the unemployed association to the Public Assistance Committee in the Town Hall. The leader was a man called George Short. Your dad said he is a communist and he is an ex miner from county Durham so I don't know why he is here in Middlesbrough. They wanted an end to the means test, free milk, free dinners and free boots for children in need, rents not to go up, private landlords to pay rates on empty houses. We can all agree with that but will they listen. I don't think so. The editor of the Gazette said the deputation were beating the air. It's all a question of who will pay and how to defeat the cheats. One man has just been sent to prison for a month for not declaring that he ran a firewood business for six weeks earning thirty shillings a week. He has a wife and four children. Nurses have just got a wage increase. Ward sisters will get £75 a year rising to £85 over two years. That's just under thirty shillings a week in the first year and just over after two years. Staff nurses get £45 and after a year £50. That's less than a pound a week for looking after people in hospital. And there's not a thing anyone can do about it. I think if the Prime Minister got what nurses get there would be a change pretty quick.

Constantine College students rag week started at the Gaumont last night when they chose Tees-side's beauty queen. Dora Craster who lives in Linthorpe Rd won it. Last year it was Ivy Peacock from 37 Coltman Street in North Ormesby. That's the street you were born in at your dad's sister's house. Our Jimmy said I would have won it last year if I had gone in for it. He still thinks that the two Pears soap advertising pictures on our front kitchen wall are me and your auntie Pam. I want to tell him that they are not and that I have been having him on but I don't know how to go about it he's so serious. I think I will leave it till he is older and we can have a laugh about it. Fingers crossed.

We've been reading about the King inspecting the fleet in the royal yacht and all the sailors lining the decks to cheer him.

You must tell me all about it. The papers say he visited the Hood and went to sea in an aircraft carrier HMS Courageous to watch naval flying. It seems a short space for aeroplanes to land on and take off. It must be very dangerous.

Did you know they have raised the bow of the submarine M2 that sank but there is a leak in the torpedo tube so they can't raise it any further just yet. And a French submarine has sank during trials. 62 men have gone down in her and seven who were on the bridge have been saved. If you ask me these submarines are very dangerous so I hope you will not volunteer.

Mrs Levinson said that she does not think there will be a war with Germany because Hitler will not be elected. I asked her what made her so sure and she said because in Lausanne, that's in Switzerland the allies have agreed not to make Germany pay reparations for the war, just 150 million pounds towards a reconstruction fund. The way she says just 150 millions as if it was a mere bagatelle astonishes me. But I suppose when you've got money it's easy to talk like that. Anyway this is one of the things that Hitler goes on about that he would end and can't anymore.

Well, I'm going to have to go. We went to Redcar at the weekend, there was a heat wave and Redcar was crowded. Down the town people brought their gramophones out into the street for entertainment it was so hot. Middlesbrough children won the inter-town elementary school sports on Redcar racecourse. That's where Paddy loses some of his money backing losers. Jimmy is out playing over the beck at least I hope it's over and not in. He's a little devil. Ta Ta Pet and Sadie ask to be remembered. Sadie was on about what shares she should sell and which she should buy. I thought she would have been tired of it by now but she gets worse. So if you have got some spare cash instead of going in a pub and drinking it the shares to buy are Mathews and Butlers Birmingham Breweries. Sadie said so. So stay sober. Tara for now,

Your everloving,

Mam

PS General celebrations here. Jack Peterson from Cardiff knocked out Reggie Meen at Wimbledon Stadium to win the heavyweight championship of Great Britain and the Lonsdale belt. The way Taffy Evans is carrying on you would think he had won it. Still it's understandable I suppose. If Peterson was English they'd have the flags out here.

Friday 22 July 1932

Dear Bob

Here I am again with me acid drops to ask how you are and hope you are enjoying life.

Mrs Levinson asked me to bake a cake for some do the Conservative Party were having. She was very pleased with it and she told me some of the complimentary things the people at the do said about it. It was very flattering. I nearly said open the window while I throw me chest out, but you can't say things like that in posh people's houses, they would think you were common, and besides it was her window. So I just glowed.

Jimmy's going through his Fe Fi Fo Fum I smell the blood of an Englishman phase. He's been trying to frighten me with no success but he's been terrifying little Sammy and Joyce next door. Mrs Walters came in to complain and ask me to stop him. I've threatened to tell his dad if I hear any more of it. That always works.

I don't know what goes through that boy's mind. The other day I noticed he was walking funny round the house. He was putting his toes down before his heels. So I asked him if there was something wrong with his feet, but he was being an Indian. He'd read a story in one of the boys magazines, the Wizard or the Rover or something, that a tracker in the forest in America said to the white men that he was tracking for that there were Indians ahead. They asked him how he knew and he pointed to foot prints in the leaves on the ground. He said they were Indian foot prints because Indians put their toes down first. Well, you should have heard him. Our mam, you've spoilt it now, and he went into the sulks. Well how was I to know he was an Indian. He didn't have a feather in his hair or a sign on his back saying I'm an Indian. I was only looking at his feet. Anyway a few minutes later he was asking for a slice of jam and bread. I suppose he thought he was entitled to compensation.

Sadie is a bit worried about what is going to happen to her folks in Ireland which is now out of the Commonwealth trade preferences so that there is a 20% tariff on imports from Ireland and they say it will be a disaster for Irish farmers. We'll just have to wait and see what Mr de Valera does. The Government wants to let Irish farmers who are tenants buy their farms for less than the rent they pay and are willing to go to arbitration. But de Valera is opposed. He has had a meeting with the Prime Minister but they came to no agreement. Some of the Irish Ministers have gone to Ottawa to take part in the talks there on trade preferences so they seem to be opposed to Mr de Valera. The Gazette says this is economic war between Britain and Ireland starting tonight with a Reprisals bill in Parliament. A move to boycott British goods has started in Dublin. Isn't it ridiculous?

There's a photo in the Gazette of some schoolboys from Islington in London on a tour of Skinningrove Ironworks and seeing a furnace being tapped. It makes you wonder who thought that up and what subject they were doing at school. There's some High School boys from here going to France to meet French and German students and to learn foreign languages. It's good to see children getting round like that and meeting others but I wonder where the money comes from. It's costing the High School boys £8 for a fortnight and we couldn't afford that.

The new bridge they are building over the river at Newport is what they call a vertical lift bridge, that means that there are two high columns one on either bank and they lift the bridge to let ships pass under on the way to Stockton. There's only one other bridge like it and that's in America. There's another achievement for Middlesbrough. Kaye Don has just smashed the world speed record with his speedboat Miss England 3 on Loch Lomond. He did 119 miles an hour. At that speed he'll be meeting himself coming back. Though why anybody wants to travel at that speed I don't understand. I suppose that's the way of the world now, the age of the horse and cart is disappearing. Freddie Dixon who has a garage on Linthorpe Road is a racing driver and he is going in the Ulster TT next month. If he wins that will be a feather in the cap for Middlesbrough's motor racing enthusiasts.

There's more trouble in Germany with Communists and Nazis fighting each other. Thousands of Nazis in uniform marched through the streets and the Communists opposed them and there was shooting and twelve people killed and lots wounded. The police attacked the Communists. I don't think political parties should be allowed to wear uniforms or carry guns. They are not armies. President Hindenburg has made the Chancellor a dictator because the Government can't govern because of all the violence. There's going to be another election and Hitler says he will be the Chancellor after the election. Hitler is flying all round Germany in an aeroplane on an election campaign. It makes you wonder where he gets the money from. It's not so long ago he was an unemployed artist. Stan Cole says that if Hitler becomes Chancellor he will make such a mess of things that the people of Germany will chuck him out and then the Communists will be elected. The way Stan talks I think he has a crystal ball. Whether it's a good one or not remains to be seen but it's let him down in the past.

Your dad and all the men who go in Stan Cole's shed were at a meeting organised by the trade unions in Middlesbrough to discuss what can be done about the state of the industry in this area and they had a Professor and Mrs Schofield Coates from here as speakers. She does a lot of this sort of thing. I wouldn't be surprised if she was an MP one day. The Professor said that we are an isolated area far from large centres of population and employers consider the transport costs. Also it is all heavy industry and men's work so there's not much for women. I don't see what there not being much work for women has to do with the steelworks and shipyards being closed down, but he is a professor so he should know what he's talking about. He also said that the only hope for the North East is new scientific discoveries coming here. Mrs Schofield Coates said the warehouses are full of goods we would like to have and if we can get them then work will follow. Everybody cheered her. So that's one up for the women. Maybe one day we will have a woman as Prime Minister and see if women can do better than the men. But not in my lifetime

Your dad and me went to the Elite to see Edward G Robinson and Loretta Young in The Honourable Mr Wong. Edward G is a respectable merchant during the day and at night is an executioner for the secret society. I won't tell you how it ends in case you get a chance to see it but they are both good actors.

Well Bob, I have to go. Duty calls. I can hear the pitter patter of his tiny feet coming in the back door. Ta Ta Pet asks to be remembered.

Tara for now,
Your everloving,
Mam

Friday 29 July 1932

Dear Bob,

How are you? The usual start but I have to ask. We got your letter from Weymouth telling us about the King inspecting the fleet in the Royal Yacht and how you only had to stand on the upper deck and cheer him. I suppose he wouldn't have time to go on every ship, going round the Hood and going to sea on the aircraft carrier HMS Courageous to watch naval air warfare would be more than enough. But thanks for telling us about it, that's the kind of letter I want that tells me lots of what you are doing. Ta Ta Pet was saying that aeroplanes will play a large part in the next war. Sometimes he talks as if there is going to be one. He was telling us that another aircraft carrier HMS Glorious had a collision with a French liner in thick fog in the Mediterranean in April last year. He'd read the court case which said the French liner was two thirds to blame for changing course across the bows of the Glorious. Twenty two people were killed on the French liner. I think he reads the Times like Mr Levinson but he probably just reads it in the library reading room. Your dad has had a letter from an old army pal who is a riveter like your dad. He lives in Devonport and a new sloop has just been launched called HMS Weston Super Mare. So he expects to be soon out of work unless the Navy orders some more ships.

It was a laugh a minute here the other night. Sadie had come in at the same time as Ta Ta Pet and started on about shares and Ta Ta Pet called her a bull. She wasn't pleased and she wanted to know what he meant. Poor old Ta Ta Pet was really in trouble and he went red and he tried to explain but Sadie wouldn't let him get in a word edgeways. She went on and on. When she'd gone home your dad said he felt sorry for Paddy. Anyway Ta Ta Pet had finally managed to explain to her why he called her a bull and it was quite interesting. Sadie had been on about shares as usual and how she was going to buy some brewery shares because their price was going to rise and then she would sell them and make a profit. That's when Ta Ta Pet called her a bull. When she'd got cooled down enough to let him speak he explained that people who think that share prices are going to rise are optimists and are called bulls on the Stock Exchange. People who think share prices are going to fall are pessimists and they are called bears.

Bears sell shares that they haven't got and when the price falls they buy and hand the shares over to the person they sold them to when they didn't have any. They make a profit by selling dear and buying cheap. Does that make sense to you.

Bulls are optimists, They think share prices are going to rise so they buy shares with money that they haven't got and when the price rises they sell them. Then they pay the person they bought shares from and pocket the difference. So they buy cheap and sell dear.

Well, Ta Ta Pet had us all baffled how bulls and bears could do this but he said that when people sell shares they don't have to hand them over until settlement day which is once every month. So Bears sell shares on the promise that they will deliver in a couple of weeks time on settlement day and they think that the price will fall before then. So your dad said well suppose the price doesn't fall but goes up. Ta Ta Pet said that in that case the Bears selling the shares in the first place would lose money. It's all a gamble he said.

Then he said a Bull buys shares with money he hasn't got. Sadie butted in and said that's me so is that why I am a bull. No he said, a Bull is called that because he is an optimist, he thinks share prices will rise. So when they have gone up he sells the shares that he bought with the money he hasn't got and pays the person he bought from with the money he gets from selling the shares. The difference is his profit. So I said well, if prices don't go up where does that leave Sadie, and Ta Ta Pet said in debt. So that's another useless piece of information I've got. But at least I know that Sadie is a bull. She doesn't look like one I have to admit. I might try asking Mrs Levinson one day when she is giving me one or her lectures on the state of the country whether her husband is a bull or a bear. But I'll have to be careful how I do it. Perhaps I'll ask her what are bulls and bears and see if she gives me a clear explanation.

There's a couple of good letters in the Gazette. At least Stan Cole thinks one of them is good because he read it out in the shed and he read it to me when he came here for your dad to go to the Cleveland. The man calls himself Equity and he is replying to a man called Dick Kennedy who had written in about people who build bridges and those who open them. Anyway this is what Mr Equity wrote.

When they pin the stars and garters
And give the titles rare
The men who earned their honours
Are the men who won't be there.

Stan has copied it out and nailed it on to the inside of the door of his shed so that when you open the door to go in you see it and when you open the door to come out you see it again.

There's another one in from a young man who came to Saltburn on holiday. He said he was attracted by the poster that said what a beautiful place Saltburn is but you can't go looking at the beauty spots day after day and night after night and he doesn't want to spend six nights at the pictures. He said that the girls have to be in bed at ten and so that is what he has had to do for three weeks. We were reading this with a gang of women in Mrs Maynards and we were in stitches. Poor lad.

I boned Stan about the Stockton Communist Party secretary a man called Kenny who was sent to prison for a month's hard labour for neglecting to maintain his wife and children. He was getting twenty two shillings a week for being out of work and he gave the landlady fifteen shillings and drank the rest giving his wife nothing. Stan said Mr Kenny was expelled from the Communist Party in January and he quoted a Mr George Short who is the district organiser of the Communist Party. He showed me the letter from Mr Short that was in the Gazette. He said he is carrying it round with him to show people because I'm not the first one to say something about it. Well Stan really took the wind out of my sails with that one.

There's more bad news about jobs here. Pease and Partners Normanby Ironworks has shut down two furnaces putting 400 men out of work. And how about this. People living in German Street in Redcar have just had the name changed to Banks Street. I wonder what came over them after all this time. Your dad wants to go to the Elite to see a German film called Kameradschaft. It's about a mine disaster in France in 1906 when 1,400 French miners lost their lives. German miners just over the border went to their rescue. When you learn about things like this and then remember the war you just wonder how things can change like that and why.

Well Bob, I'll have to go. I could sit here all day talking to you, or writing to you, but duty calls. I can hear him.

Tara for now and look after yourself. Everybody asks to be remembered.

Your everloving,
Mam

Friday 5 August 1932

Dear Bob,

I am absolutely blazing. I just sat down to write this letter when I heard the coalman in our street then I saw him pass, so I thought I would go out and see if his horse had done anything and it had, right outside our gate. So I came in to get our bucket and shovel and when I went out Mrs Smithers was there shoveling the last bit into her bucket. She must have run down the street to get there before me. She seemed a bit jumpy when she saw me with my bucket and shovel. I don't know whether she was just feeling guilty or she thought I was going to doll her with my shovel, because she said "it's a nice day". Well I knew it was a nice day. I didn't need her to tell me it was a nice day. Then she said this is good for the rhubarb. Well I didn't need her to tell me that either. I know it's good for the rhubarb but our rhubarb never gets a look in with her around. I don't know how she knows but she seems to have some kind of sixth sense with horses. I wouldn't be surprised if you looked back into her family history there wasn't a horse in there somewhere. Probably kept them in the kitchen. So I'm really blazing though that's not how I meant to start.

How are you? I suppose you are still in Devonport. What is it like down there? It is hard to imagine anything different from here with all the steelworks blast furnaces and foundries and shipyards. I wonder what people there do for a living. I know what at present we do up here. Draw the dole or the pancrack. I was reading in the Gazette the Durham County Corporation's budget for 1933. Forty one per cent of the population are out of work. They spend £1,454,155 on elementary education and £1,294,617 on public assistance. And on top of that you have to add what is being paid out to people on the dole by the Government. The Government has given Middlesbrough Public Assistance Committee a telling off for being too generous in the way they are applying the means test. You might not understand this, I didn't till it was explained to me. There is a thing called transitional payment that is paid for by the Government to people whose dole has run out and are not yet on public assistance. The public assistance committee have to decide how much it will be. And the Government is saying that Middlesbrough public assistance committee are making the transitional payments too high. They have to make it the same as they would give to people on public assistance. Well Councillor Tommy Meehan didn't take kindly to that and he said that if we don't do what the Government want us to do they will do it for us, so the solution is to increase the amount we give in public assistance to the amount that we are giving in transitional payment then the two will be in line. Cutting the transitional payment would cost the unemployed three shillings and three pence a week. I didn't understand all this and there was a gang of us discussing it in our house.

Anyway, the council are proposing to increase the amount they give to people on public assistance, what we call the pancrack, from ten shillings a week for a single man age 18-21 living at home to twelve shillings and sixpence and over 21 from twelve shillings and sixpence to fifteen shillings and three pence. A man and a wife with one child will get their money increased from twenty four shillings to twenty five shillings and three pence and with two children from twenty seven shillings to twenty seven shillings and three pence. The Government is saying this is too much. The pancrack should not be increased and the transitional payment should be reduced to the same as the pancrack.

Sadie said what a good man Tommy Meehan is and that he is a catholic. Sadie's very religious. Well you know what Stan Cole thinks of religion so he said he didn't care if Tommy Meehan was a Red Indian. And just then one of Ta Ta Pet's bicycle clips sprang off his leg right into the middle of our mat. Well everybody looked at it and Sadie crossed herself and said bejaysus that's a sign from God and we were all wondering how it happened so Jock Muir picked it up and said Sheffield steel. Everybody knows that Sheffield steel is not as good as ours. So that was his explanation. Ta Ta Pet had gone red and they asked him if he could do it again but there was no explanation except Sadie's. Anyway the council turned down Mr Meehan's proposal. I think the Government had them frightened. Councillor Carter said they could save on the rates if Councillors' allowances were reduced and if they travelled third class instead of first class on the railway.

Two 18 year old youths here have been sent to Borstal for three years for breaking into a gas meter and stealing one shilling and seven pence. It seems harsh but they were on probation already. I wonder what will become of them.

I'm reading the news from America and I just don't know what to make of it. War veterans marched in Washington to demand their war bonus (whatever that is) be paid to them now and they were joined by unemployed people and President Hoover turned the army on them with fixed bayonets and tanks and tear gas. The unemployed had made a camp outside Washington and the army attacked that and there were women and children in it. The American Government says they weren't all genuine ex servicemen, some of them were communists. There was a march by the Middlesbrough Unemployed Workers' Movement here to Redcar yesterday but it rained heavily and only a few turned up your dad said.

There's been an election in Germany and the Nazis got the most votes and the most seats in Parliament, more than the socialists and the communists put together but there are a lot of other parties and the Nazis have not got a majority over them all. They are furious and they have been attacking communists' homes and socialist newspapers with guns and bombs. They say that the Chancellor will be the same one they have already a man called von Papen who doesn't belong to any party and he will rule like a dictator until there is another election that settles it one way or the other. I asked Stan Cole why the communists and socialists don't join together to fight the Nazis instead of fighting each other but he says the socialists are no good. He still thinks that if Hitler gets power he will make such a mess of things that the German people will kick him out and vote for the communists.

There's a very funny letter in the Gazette. There's a man signed himself Felix criticising Saltburn. He was supporting what that other lad who had come to Saltburn for his holidays had written about Saltburn. So a man who has signed himself Can Dance has written in supporting Saltburn. He says Felix had written that Saltburn Council ought to liven the place up a bit and Can Dance says Felix wants people to run around to amuse him. He says Felix has done too much walking and he could hire a car or he could hire hard up people like himself to wheel him about in a bath chair for a moderate fee. I don't know how they think them up.

There's another letter asking if Middlesbrough football club couldn't reduce the price for the unemployed because a shilling is too much. I thought that was a good idea but your dad said that if they did that they would find that the only people going to the match were unemployed, or saying they were. There's nowt so queer as folks as the saying goes.

Well Bob, I'll have to go. Your dad will be in soon. Jimmy and his pals are over the beck so there will be a bit of peace for a while. He'll probably come in black as the ace of spade and then I will have to make him confront his mortal enemy, soap. There'll be some squalls about that. There's no PS till the football starts and it is too complicated to try work out what is happening in the Olympic games in America. There are so many different events. So tara for now. Everybody asks to be remembered.

Your everloving,

Mam.

Friday 12 August 1932

Dear Bob,

How are you? I have to ask though I am finding it hard to concentrate. Our Jimmy and some of his pals went to Redcar last Saturday and they went to Sunshine Corner on the sands and it's been purgatory ever since. He sings that song over and over again.

Sunshine Corner oh it's jolly fine
It's for children under ninety nine
All are welcome
Seats are given free
Redcar Sunshine Corner is the place for me.

I've had to write the words down to try and get them out of my system. Something like the hair of the dog. Even when I go to bed the words are going through my head. The Gazette says there were two thousand people turned up to hear Cousin Tom's Happy Sunbeams singing hymns. Well, I'm having to listen to Jimmy and his pals and Happy Sunbeam is not what is running through my mind. Last year there was a dog used to turn up and join in and when the singing finished he used to trot off. I wish I could just trot off to escape Jimmy who is in continuous rehearsals for the next time he goes.

Stan Cole and a couple of the other fellas from his shed were in for your dad to go to the Cleveland. They don't get much further these days. They find it hard to pass the door. My father boozes mainly in the Newport area with them living in Carlow Street. His regular is the Newport Working Men's Club, but many a time when I was a girl I had to meet him outside a pub where he'd stopped on his way home from work to get his wages for my mother. The County on Newport Rd was one of his favourites and I always had to meet him there, but he liked the Acklam and the Princess Alice on Newport Rd and the Volunteer and the Cannon on Cannon Street. I think it depended on his mood or who he was coming home with which pub he went in. Your dad's sitting in the corner with his nose in his dictionary and I just asked him to remind me of the name of the pubs on Cannon Street and he wanted to know why. So I told him and now he wants me to tell you about the pubs he used to go in when he was living in North Ormesby and the different pubs him and his mates used to go in when they went on a pub crawl in the boro. They would meet in the Pennymans Arms in North Ormesby market place then go to the Cuckoo in Smeaton Street. He told me it got the name of the cuckoo because there was a cuckoo clock in the bar. Lots of people didn't have clocks in those days and so when they wanted to know the time they would go down to the pub and look at the clock through the window. Next stop would be the Borough then on to the Leeds, the Central, the Wellington, and over the railway to the Criterion, the Fleece, the Robin Hood, the Vane Arms, the Steam Packet and The Ship. I told him to stop there. I think he's having me on, in fact I know he's having me on, and here I am writing them all down like an idiot when all the time he's having me on telling me the names of all the pubs in the borough he can think of when I could be writing something useful, though I suppose he would say this is useful information for you when you come home and you can see the pubs that your dad went in.. Anyway I've written them down now so I am not starting again.

Sadie's sister Kathleen was here last week. She is a teacher and lives in London. She isn't married because if she got married she would get the sack. Women teachers are not allowed to get married. Anyway one day Sadie took Kathleen down to Welford Street off Cannon Street to show where she used to live before she came to Grove Hill. Then they went and looked in St Patrick's church then at the new bridge that is being built over the river at Newport and in the afternoon they went to the Scala.

Next day Sadie asked me to go with them to show Kathleen Fairy Dell and Primrose Valley. We called in the hut at the bottom of Saltersgill lane and had a herb beer shandy. On the way back we went in Marton bungalow for a cup of tea and a cake. Kathleen was paying all the time because we had nothing. The next day we caught a bus to Ayton and went up Roseberry Topping and then we had a cup of tea and a cake in Ayton while we were waiting for the bus back. The next day we caught a bus to Redcar and walked along the sands to Marske where we had a cup of tea and a sandwich. Then a bus home. So altogether Kathleen had a good tour of the area. Of course there's a lot more to see like Eston nab but there wasn't time.

One night Sadie and Kathleen went to the Palladium. They asked me but I didn't have any money and I felt that I had cost Kathleen enough already.

Sadie brought Kathleen over to our house to meet Ta Ta Pet but what she didn't reckon with was that Ta Ta Pet would start talking about shares. As soon as she had introduced Kathleen he said there is a good share to buy, W G Clarke who make dog biscuits and other animal food. The dividend is only six per cent but the price of their one pound shares on the market is only fourteen shillings and sixpence. So if Sadie bought now she could sell when the price goes up. So Sadie said she would sell her International Tea shares and buy some Clarke shares. Ta Ta Pet asked her how many International Tea shares she would sell so she said two thousand. Ta Ta Pet looked astonished but then Sadie started counting on her fingers and said make that three thousand. Ta Ta Pet looked amazed. He knew that Sadie really didn't have any shares but he had never known how many shares it was that she didn't have. He'd thought in terms of two or three not two or three thousand. Kathleen looked amazed as well and she said you never told me you had some shares. Sadie had never thought to tell her about the shares she buys and sells in her dreams so she told Kathleen she would explain when they got home. I would have liked to have been in on that conversation. Anyway it was nice to meet Kathleen. She's the only one of Sadie's family that I've met.

It's Teesside's holiday week next week but seeing your dad is out of work it won't make any difference to us. One of the shipyards he has worked in, Furness's at Haverton Hill is closing down for two weeks because there is so little work. Sir Graham Bower who was in the navy for twenty three years has been telling the story that in 1914 two German cruisers stopped some British liners with women and children on board and told the captains if they would destroy their wireless sets they could go. He said if there is a roll of honour for the heroes of international law the names of those two captains should be put on it. It goes to show that the Germans are no different to us.

Rin Tin Tin has died in Hollywood. Remember how you used to like that dog. He was very clever.

I've just been reading in the Gazette that the old shelter near the Canon lake in Albert Park has been pulled down and a new one put in its place. The Gazette says it was known as the old man's Parliament because men used to go there to discuss the affairs of the day. Well the Gazette needn't worry because I can tell them where there still is one. Stan Cole's shed.

The news from Germany is very worrying. Nazi ammunition dumps have been found and in the past ten weeks 130 people have been killed. They even threw a bomb through the bedroom window of the leader of the socialist party.

Fortunately nobody was in. And bricks are being thrown through Jews' shop windows. I just don't understand where they think this gets them and how they would govern. I tell myself that the people won't vote for them yet they get over 13 million votes. We had some trouble here the other day but nothing like Germany. There was a demonstration of unemployed outside the Town Hall. Some of them were allowed in but when they insisted on speaking at the council meeting the police threw them out. They said that the Public Assistance Committee are bluffing them because they have increased outdoor relief to the same as transitional payments benefits but this has to be approved by the Minister of Labour and they know he won't approve. Transitional benefit is what men get when their dole runs out and before they go on to public assistance which comes out of the rates.

Well that's something about Germany and here but what about this from America. An Englishman Mr Hall went to Chicago to give a lecture on English literature. When he got off the train he was met by some women teachers who had not been paid for a year. The hall was crowded for his lecture and at the end a Chicago gangster called Spike Mulligan sent up his card. Mr Hall thought he was going to demand protection money but he invited him up to the stage. Mr Mulligan said "Say, I'm right glad to meet ya. Don't mind me stepping up but I'd like to know more about this guy Charles Dickens" He invited Mr Hall to his home which was built in Spanish style with a musician's gallery and two butlers to wait on them while they were eating. So then, according to Mr Hall he said to Mr Mulligan aren't you ashamed of yourself, and he said "Ashamed? It's not my fault. I'd like to be honest but if I quitted the racket they'd kill me. When I entered this business I didn't know it was going to lead to this and now I'd like to be out of it but what do I do. The police are grafters, the politicians are grafters. I pity those school kids having to go without their feed because the burgh's bankrupt. I make contributions to the relief fund every now and then but you can't make a habit of it." And then he said that the new racket, kidnapping is wrong.

So there we have it, Germany, Britain and America. So who am I supposed to vote for? I'll have to go, Sadie's just walked in and I can hear the happy sunbeam coming through the back door.

Your dad and me are going to the Palladium to see the comedian Sydney Howard in Splinters in the Navy which is about life on a battleship. You can guess why.

Tara for now. Everybody asks to be remembered.
Your everloving,
Mam

Friday 19 August 1932

Dear Bob,

Just to ask you how you are and to tell you the latest. I was crossing the road to Mrs Maynards when Mrs Callender came walking down the street with her fur collar on. She stopped me to chat and I wondered why but I soon found out. You like my fur collar she said, I've noticed you looking at it. Well I had to say I had and I asked her if it keeps her warm. I was just being polite really but she said it does you would be surprised how much it keeps you warm. She asked me why I don't get one. Well she knows why I don't get one, I can't afford it, so I nearly asked her how much hers was but I thought better of it. I know that her sister in London sent her it. She doesn't know that I know but Ta Ta Pet found out for me but I couldn't tell her that. Anyway she got round to what she was leading up to. "You think this fur collar is something but just wait till you see Mrs Quinn's fur coat". What fur coat, I said. Sadie hasn't got a fur coat. "Not yet she hasn't" said Mrs Callender, "but just wait, she can't keep all that money in the bank for ever. She'll spend some of it sometime" What money, I said. "Her legacy" she said, "she must have told you about it you being so close." So I said Sadie had never told me about her legacy, which was true, because she hadn't got a legacy and was I regretting ever telling Ta Ta Pet that she had just so he wouldn't know she was pulling his leg when she was talking about selling her gilts. Anyway that was that. She had made her point and she was on her way. I think she was going to Mrs Turnbull's. They are very thick, I think they get together round a glass of Mrs Turnbull's rhubarb wine and work out who's doing what round here.

Anyway I went to see Mrs Maynard and I didn't think any more about it then in the afternoon there was a knock at our front door. It was Mrs Hall from down the street. I was surprised because she has never been in our house, we are not that close but I asked her in. She wanted to borrow a quarter of tea. She said she'd just realised she was out of it and Mr Hall would be coming in soon. Anyway I said I couldn't lend her a quarter but I could lend her a few teaspoons to keep her going and she said that would do. So I put a few teaspoonfuls in some paper and I was screwing it up when she said "Have you heard. Mrs Quinn is getting a fur coat." Well I had heard, from Mrs Callender just that morning but I wasn't going to let on that I had. So I just said get away, Sadie couldn't afford a fur coat. Where would she get the money from. "From her legacy" sez Mrs Hall. "Hasn't she told you about it." Well of course I said that she hadn't. "Well" sez Mrs Hall, "when her mother died in Ireland they found a large sum of money under her bed. Thousands they say". Thousands, I said, her mother was poor and lived on a farm. Where would she get thousands from? "Well they do say it was from a bank robbery." I could have fallen through the floor. When I told Ta Ta Pet that Sadie had a legacy from her mother who'd died I didn't say anything about them finding thousands of pounds under her death bed or a bank robbery. Honestly, the way people make things up round here they could drive you mad.

Me telling Ta Ta Pet that Sadie had a legacy, which I only did for the best of reasons has gone all wrong. As Mr Muir would say, the best laid plans of mice and men gang aft aglee. I don't know whether that is the way to spell it but that's how he says it. Whenever anything goes wrong Jock says "Ah weel, as oor Rabbie wad say, the best laid plans of mice and men gang aft aglee". Mrs Muir told me Jock has a copy of Robert Burns poetry and he is always reading it, something like your dad always reading his dictionary I suppose. Well, anyway, my best laid plan, not that I planned it, it just came out somehow, has definitely gone aglee, and I don't know whether I should tell Sadie or just hope that it will go away. I think I'll wait. When she doesn't buy a fur coat people might twig that it was not true about her legacy and it will fade away.

There's been fighting in Spain between republicans and those who want the monarchy back but it has ended and the general who started it has been arrested. Some people think that if they get rid of the King their problems will be over but look at America, they're a republic, they don't have a king and look what it's like there. Mind you, we have a king and look what it's like here.

I was talking to Ta Ta Pet some time ago about the poem Crossing the Bar and how it means to sailors that if somebody has crossed the bar it means that they have died. And now there is an interesting article in the Gazette about it by the Reverend Hodgson. He says that Lord Tennyson wrote the poem when he was on holiday in Salcombe in Devon and he went for a cruise on Lord Brassey's yacht Sunbeam. As they crossed the bar a church bell was ringing for evensong and that inspired the poem. The poem is sung as a hymn, although I've never heard it, and an artist painted the scene. I would like to see it. I thought this would be of interest to you seeing that you are a sailor and you are still in Devonport. It might inspire you. It's a lovely poem and I am copying it out for you. I have a feeling I've sent it to you before but just to make sure here it is.

Crossing the Bar

Sunset and evening star,
And one clear call for me!
And may there be no moaning of the bar,
When I put out to sea,

But such a tide as moving seems asleep,
Too full for sound and foam,
When that which drew from out the boundless deep
Turns again home.

Twilight and evening bell,
And after that the dark!
And may there be no sadness of farewell,
When I embark;

For though from out our bourne of Time and Place
The flood may bear me far,
I hope to see my Pilot face to face
When I have crossed the bar.

You think of something like this that a human being can write and then you read what the IRA did to a farmer in Ulster. They took all his clothes off then covered him in tar from head to foot then tied him up with wire and left him in a field all night. Another farmer found him the next morning. You wonder what goes through people's minds that they can do that to another human being. Mr de Valera has ordered four thousand tons of coal from Poland as a part of the trade war with Britain. Where is it all going to end. The Irish are no different to us and there are lots of Irish in Middlesbrough. In fact a lot of streets are named after parts of Ireland, Carlow Street where we come from, Kildare Street and that's just two.

Your granddad and grandma went to Redcar with the Newport Working Men's club outing. Newport railway station

was opened specially and every child under fourteen was given sixpence. Now that's a club to be in but we live too far away.
Well Bob I'm going on too long so on that happy note I will close. No sign of the jam and bread kid. I wonder what's wrong.
Tara for now,
Your everloving,
Mam

Friday 26 August 1932

Dear Bob,

Here I am with my weekly epistle asking how you are and hoping that you are fine. You seem to be spending a lot of time in Devonport, not that I am objecting, but couldn't you ask the captain to bring the ship up to Middlesbrough just for a change.

Your auntie Edie and uncle John were here the other night. He was going to go to the Cleveland with your dad and some of the other fellas. He's very quiet and he doesn't drink much but he likes to go out with your dad now and again. He works at the Britannia and as they still live down Gladstone Street they left their bairns with your grandma in Carlow Street and they would sleep there the night so John could go out with your dad. Then Ta Ta Pet came in and he hadn't been in long when Sadie came in. She must have been watching out for Ta Ta Pet so she could talk about shares but she missed your auntie Edie and uncle John. You might remember I told you about the last time your auntie Edie was here and Sadie and me played a prank on her and Sadie came in and talked in a posh accent. Well, when your auntie Edie saw Sadie she said Hello, you're the posh lady from Cannon Street. I met you the last time I was here. We'd explained to her that we were only having her on so now she was having her own back. Ta Ta Pet and your dad didn't know about this of course so they were looking at her wondering what was going on. Your uncle John was looking at her as well, in fact he couldn't take his eyes off her. Luckily your auntie Edie was sitting between him and Sadie so she couldn't see the expression on his face. If she had of done she would have been out of our house like a shot with your uncle John in tow. But after a few minutes Sadie said she didn't realise we had company and she left. Well then your auntie Edie explained how Sadie had kidded her up with her cut glass accent so we all had a laugh about that.

Your dad and your uncle John went to the Cleveland and when they came back they brought fish and chips. After your auntie Edie and uncle John had gone home I asked your dad what John had thought about Sadie. He said he was smitten. So I said how do you know, what did he say, so your dad said he didn't say anything, so I said well if he didn't say anything how do you know and he said that's how I know. Well they say still waters run deep and your dad is down there with the best of them.

That man Hitler in Germany is terrible. Nine members of his Nazi party broke into a communist's house and beat him unconscious then shot him dead in front of his mother. They were arrested and sentenced to death and Hitler has sent a telegram to President Hindenberg demanding that they be pardoned. This man's party gets thirteen million votes. I was round at Mrs Levinson's to do the cleaning and she had the tea and ginger biscuits out, I think I told you that she says that ginger biscuits set the brain on fire. She said that the reason he gets so many votes is that he has wrapped the German flag round him and blames all Germany's woes on the allies who beat Germany in the war and he says he will abolish the Versailles Treaty Germany had to sign at the end of the war and Germany will not pay reparations for the war and they will have as big an army as anybody else. She said this is what to expect from Hitler and his party and if they ever get here they will be murdering their opponents just like they are in Germany now, that's why we should be re-arming. I was reading that the Prince of Wales and Prince George are in the Mediterranean watching the fleet exercising. They went up in aeroplanes from HMS Glorious and then they watched two battleships HMS Revenge and HMS Queen Elizabeth in a mock battle at night with some county class cruisers like the one you are on as the enemy. Your dad said the cruisers wouldn't stand a chance against the battleships' heavy guns once the battleships fired star shell to light them up. It makes me feel a bit safer knowing that if Hitler does get power in Germany and declares war that he has to get past the Navy. Then I think of the cost of it all, not that Stan Cole will ever let me forget and I read people complaining in the letters page in the Gazette. A single man has written in that he gets seven shillings and sixpence a week from the Public Assistance Committee and has to pay four shillings a week rent for a room. He has been away in the army for eight years and is now in the reserve so he gets reserve pay quarterly and the Public Assistance Committee say he is being overpaid. It just seems all so impossible.

There's a column called Flashlights in the Gazette and the writer Mr Thomas Jay says that there is a man in Belfast who is 101 years old and he says that he puts it down to him drinking a pint of stout every day for the last 63 years and the teetotalers over there are saying it will get him eventually. How do they know? I suppose Bertie Gibson the head lad of the Sons of Temperance will agree with them. I'll have to ask him and see what he says. And Mr Jay says that things are now so bad that when a burglar breaks into somebody's house all they get is practice. That's certainly all that he'd get here, unless your dad caught him.

Stan Cole was in laughing his head off because the Labour Party in Middlesbrough and in Hartlepool have split and so have the Independent Labour Party. He said that's because they've got no political principles to hold them together. I didn't even know there was an Independent Labour Party, I thought they were all one.

The Passionate Plumber is on the Palladium. How do they think them up? I said to your dad, the passionate plumber's on the Palladium and he said oh aye and what's he doing there. They got a leak or something. Honestly, your dad's imagination.

Well Bob, must go. I think I'll take a look at our taps and see if we need any new washers. Everybody asks to be remembered. So tara for now.

Your everloving,

Mam

PS. I've just remembered. Some time ago I told you that I had been reading about American gangsters and they talked about pineapple tossers and I wondered what they were. Well there's an American who writes dictionaries and he has included some of the gangsters' sayings. A pineapple is a bomb. I'd wondered why gangsters would be throwing pineapples and who they would be throwing them at. They could throw a pineapple at me any day. So now I know. Your dad wants a PS. He says Carnera lost on points to a Polish boxer in America and Freddie Dixon the Middlesbrough motor racing driver won the Ulster Grand Prix breaking the track record at over 74 mph. How's that for a PS. He's fallen back exhausted into his chair and disappeared behind his dictionary.

Friday 2 September 1932

Dear Bob,

How are you. I see you are still in Devonport. Is there no chance of you coming home on leave? Thank you for telling me that I had already sent you the poem Crossing the Bar. I completely forgot with reading about how it came to be written.

Geordie Henderson came walking down the street with Jock Muir when some of us women were stood gassing at our gate and Jock got on about Robbie Burns song My love is like a red red rose. So that got Geordie going and he said what about The Waters of Tyne. So we said how does that go so he sang it. The melody is beautiful. I wish Middlesbrough had songs like it. Here's the words so that you can learn them and when you come home I will teach you the tune. You need to have something that you can sing for a party piece.

The Waters of Tyne

I cannae get to my love if I would dee
The waters of Tyne run between him and me
And here I must stand with a tear in my e'e
Both sighing and sickly my sweetheart to see

Oh where is the boatman, my bonnie hinny
Oh where is the boatman - oh bring him to me
To ferry me over the Tyne to my honey
And I will remember the boatman and thee

Oh bring me a boatman, I'll gi'e all my money
And you for your trouble rewarded shall be
To ferry me over the Tyne to my honey
Or scull him across the rough river to me

Mrs Rawlins has just gone by with her bag of apples and sugar to make toffee apples and toffee umbrellas. And Mrs Callender has just gone by and she's not wearing her fox fur. I wonder if she's sickening for something.

Our Jimmy's come in and he is leaning with his elbow on the table and his head in his hand and his legs crossed and asked me what I am doing so I've said I am writing a letter so he's said who to so I said to your brother. So he said, our Bob, and I said you've only got one brother. So he said tell him I think about him. It was touching the way he said it. Then he said and I will think about him even more when I get a slice of jam and bread. Honestly. Where our Jimmy stands I picture a big hole and I'm forever shoveling slices of jam and bread into it.

Some more on the history of Middlesbrough. Sadie has been reading about the origins of the Holy Rood. It started out with Teresa Newcomen in 1854. She built Christ Church in Coatham, that's Redcar, and founded the Christ Church Sisterhood which helped the sick poor and did other works of mercy. Then there was a big accident at Snowden's works and there wasn't a hospital in Middlesbrough so a gentleman gave the money to build one in Dundas Mews. It was the first cottage hospital in England. That became North Ormesby Cottage Hospital, I used to work there as a ward maid. That's how I met your dad because he lived not far from the hospital in Alfred Street. Then the sisters became the sisters of the Holy Rood. And here we are.

Mrs Levinson had the ginger biscuits out the other day. She's really worried now about what is going on in Germany. Mr Levinson has just been to Germany on business and. he told Mrs Levinson it is getting really dangerous there. Nazis and communists have been in gun battles with each other and there is danger of civil war. She told me Mr Levinson speaks German and he was in military intelligence during the war, so he's not so green as he's cabbage looking. When I told your dad he said maybe he wasn't in Germany just on business. Anyway the German Government is saying that they should have an army of 300,000 men, tanks, artillery, battleships, battle cruisers and submarines. Mrs Levinson said her husband told her that the German battleships if they are allowed to get them will be modern while ours are not and we are cutting our navy programme of new ships to three cruisers. The Gazette says Germany will have to have an army but they won't be a threat to anyone because they have so many internal problems. Mrs Levinson used to be sure that the politicians in Germany could keep Hitler under control even if he got power but now she's not so sure and she told me to tell my communist friend that. I think she meant Stan Cole but I've never told her about Stan Cole so how she knows I don't know. Stan says that even if Hitler gets power he will soon be kicked out. I think Mrs Levinson must see me as a messenger to the working class. I know her sister thinks I'm the cat's whiskers and Mrs Levinson said she is coming up here shortly for a couple of weeks. Then maybe I'll get a chance to try her out on Dracula's dance.

Remember I told you about those five Nazis who murdered a communist and they were sentenced to death and Hitler said they had to be pardoned. He said why should five Germans be executed for one Polish peasant. Well they've been let off the death sentence and have been given hard labour for life in prison instead. Stan Cole is furious and talks about the German capitalist class supporting Hitler.

Well that's enough of the politics for one day. It's all politics round here with Stan Cole's shed and all the fellas that get in there. Then your granddad arrives and it's all the Liberal Party and how free trade is the solution to our problems. Then Ta Ta Pet comes in with his on the one hand this and on the other hand that and then on the other hand. I don't know how many hands he's got. And now Sadie's got some kind of bug about shares. I wouldn't care she'll never own a share in her life but she goes on about what she is going to buy and what she is going to sell and Ta Ta Pet encourages her. She's just been in and on about the London Brick company which is paying 20% dividend so she's going to discuss with Ta Ta Pet what she should sell to buy some London Brick shares. She just finished talking about that and she said there used to be cannibals in Cleveland. You know, I mean, there's no connection between London Brick company shares and cannibalism in Cleveland. Apart from Sadie. Anyway it seems that somebody has found some old charred human bones which proves that there used to be cannibals in Cleveland.

Your dad was out with Sam Maynard last night catching rabbits. I'm on tenterhooks until they get back. Mind you it's good to have the rabbits but it is risky. We have PC Masterman as our policeman and Sam always gives Mrs Masterman a rabbit or two but we can't rely on PC Masterman all the time. Mr Craster and Mr Cook out of Woodville Ave have just been in court. Two plain clothes policemen on duty in Grove Hill caught them at two o clock in the morning pushing a motor bike combination with 33 rabbits and nets. They said they had the permission of the farmer on Kader Close farm up Acklam but he denied it. He said he had given Mr Craster's cousin permission to clear a warren and when it was cleared that was the end of it. They were fined fifty shillings each. How could they afford fifty shillings, that's two pounds ten shillings, a week's wage for a tradesman. And if the farmer's farm was

cleared of rabbits how could Mr Craster and Mr Cook catch 33 rabbits. That's justice for you.
Well Bob, I'll have to go. Jimmy's gone out with his jam and bread
Everybody asks to be remembered. Tara for now. Look after yourself. Thanks again for reminding me about Crossing the Bar. I'll just have to get my head looked at.
Your everloving,
Mam
PS Boro 0 Aston Villa 2. So away we go for another season. On Wednesday Newcastle 5 Boro 1

Friday 9 September 1932

Dear Bob,

How are you. We received your letter saying you are still in Devonport. That's a long time, I think they could have given you some leave to come home the time you've been there.

There was such a commotion in the street just before I started writing this letter that I looked out the window and it was Dracula riding down the street with Gyp barking and snapping at his leg. He has a sit up and beg bike, Dracula not Gyp, and he was sitting straight upright with his hands on the handlebars looking straight in front pedaling with his right leg and not looking at Gyp but trying to kick him with his left leg. Mrs Callaghan, Gyp's her dog, was telling me that every time that he chases Dracula she gives him a biscuit as a treat. But if he chases anybody else he doesn't get anything.

Did I tell you about Mr Harold Davidson the Rector of Stiffkey which I have not invented. It's in Norfolk. The Norwich church authorities were investigating charges against his moral character. A landlady said she found him and a girl in the dark in a room of her house. He is accused of bribing the girl and getting her drunk. He says he was trying to help her find a job. He admitted giving her £2 and taking her into a pub but that was because it was a Sunday evening and it was foggy and he had to take her somewhere. He was found guilty of immoral conduct with young women. The next thing I read about him was a court case in Blackpool. He was running out of money to pay his legal bills so he agreed to be put on show in Blackpool sitting in a barrel and people had to pay two pence to go in the exhibition and see him. A showman Mr Gannon put the Rector of Stiffkey in one barrel to watch over a young woman in another barrel who was fasting for ten days and was being paid £200. The police said this was causing a public nuisance because a crowd of over a thousand people had gathered outside the exhibition. So Mr Gannon had to call the exhibition off but the Rector of Stiffkey is going to sit on a chair in Mr Gannon's shop and people will pay to go in and walk past him. Mr Gannon said he has had offers from round the country to put the Rector on show and the Rector says he has had film offers.

I wouldn't mind sitting on a chair and letting people pay to walk past me. In fact I stand at our gate every day and people walk past and don't pay a penny.

I find this so disgraceful. People are destitute and there are people who can afford to pay to see the Rector of Stiffkey sitting in a barrel. People in India are existing on less than twopence a day while people in Blackpool pay twopence to look at the Rector of Stiffkey sitting in a barrel. Everything seems to be topsy turvy. When your dad and me go to the cemetery to put flowers on our Mary's grave I pray to God and your dad curses the Government. And we were both brought up in the Church of England. I understand the way your dad feels but that doesn't make it easier for me. I call the Government as well but I have faith as well while your dad seems to have lost his. If we don't have faith in something what have we got and what are we? I hope that when I cross the bar that I will see my pilot face to face like in the poem and your dad when he crosses the bar.

HMS Hood has arrived in Hartlepool for Hartlepool's naval week. She's here till next Wednesday and the public are allowed on board to see her. They say the Hood is our biggest battle cruiser. Is that right? I would like to go but it is too far. Why don't they bring warships to Middlesbrough? Haven't they heard of us in London?

Remember I told you somebody said there used to be cannibals in this area because charred human bones had been found at Eston Nab. Well somebody else has written in the Gazette that there weren't any cannibals in this area because the people were civilised and there was plenty of things to eat and the charred human bones would have been of people who were caught in fires in their grass huts and burned to death. Well I'm pleased to know that because I've been looking at Dracula when he comes down Sunnyside and wondering. He looks the type.

Sherlock Holmes would have a field day if he was here trying to sort out what is happening. I asked my Dear Watson sitting in the corner with his nose in his dictionary to explain it all to me but he smiles, that's all he says. It's a lofty kind of a smile that says that he knows but only those who inhabit the heights of working class politics could possibly understand, like those who go in Stan Cole's shed, and it's not something that a pretty face like mine should bother about. Well I don't mind him telling me I have a pretty face, the oftener the better, but it's the suggestion that there isn't a brain behind it that gets me going. The Independent Labour Party in Middlesbrough has closed itself down and some of its members are going to support the Labour Party and some are not. Their candidate in St Hilda's ward said it is not the right time for a socialist movement just now, whereas Stan Cole says it is. They've split in Scotland as well and formed a new party, the Scottish Socialist Party. The way they're going on there'll soon be a socialist party for every day of the week and two on Sunday. Stan has faith in the working class, though not in me. I'm the wrong sort of working class.

There's a club been opened by the Unemployed Workers Movement where for a penny a week the members can play all sorts of games like billiards and dominoes and they have a football team. That sounds good as a way of occupying men's time. But they held an open air meeting in South Bank at Bennett's corner and the speaker was dragged from the platform by the crowd. He managed to escape but he was chased through the streets and only saved himself by running into a police station. The police then gave him an escort to the bus back to Middlesbrough. That's the working class that Stan has faith in. What with your dad going at me to be Labour, your granddad going at me to be a Liberal and Mrs Levinson going at me to be Conservative I think about politics a lot especially when I'm in bed and your dad is snoring beside me. It seems odd that during the day your dad is discussing politics in Stan Cole's shed and I'm not, and at night I'm thinking about politics and he's snoring his head off. There's a message there somewhere.

Well Bob, I'll have to go. There's so much going on. There's been big Labour Party meetings here and in Billingham where the speakers have been calling Ramsay MacDonald a traitor and saying the way to get rid of unemployment is shorter working hours and higher wages.. And to get rid of Ramsay

MacDonald and his government of course. I tell you there's a lot of confusion about.

I'll have to go, I hear the patter of tiny feet coming in through the back door. Everybody asks to be remembered.

So tara for now,

Your everloving

Mam.

PS Manchester City 2 Boro 3. Your dad said I have to tell you that Camsell has found his form again and is definitely not on the transfer list.

Friday 16 September 1932

Dear Bob,

Thanks for writing back to say that HMS Hood is our biggest battle cruiser which is what I had heard. The crew seem to be having a good time at Hartlepool, they've played a football match to raise money for Hartlepool hospital, had a dance in the Borough Hall and gave a searchlight display. Now HMS Renown another of our battle cruisers is at Whitby. There's a photograph in the Gazette of visitors being shown round the ship by the crew. You tell the captain of your ship that I want her to come to Middlesbrough so that you can show me round.

There's a big argument in the Gazette about who is responsible for the means test. One reader is saying that Mr Greenwood who was a Minister in the Labour Government sent a letter to all the Boards of Guardians telling them that when they were working out how much relief to give they had to take into account every source of income available to the family including earnings of widows and children. The reader says that is the basis of the means test so it's no good blaming the national government, it's the Labour Government's fault.

One Middlesbrough councillor, Councillor Carter has said that they could save money on the rates by reducing the mayor's salary from £500 to £350 a year, and councillors traveling and hotel expenses from one pound eleven and sixpence a day to one pound. He also said that they should travel third class like MPs have to instead of first class. And anyway he said that a lot of the conferences that councillors attend are a waste of time and he speaks from experience.

I told you about the Middlesbrough Independent Labour Party members closing their branch down. Well now most of the officials of the Middlesbrough Labour Party have resigned because their national headquarters would not agree with their selection of a candidate for the election. Some of them are big names in the Labour Party, I know they are big because I've heard of them like Mr Harford and Mr Manton. So it's all fun and games and your granddad and Mrs Levinson are loving it. So is Stan Cole which means that they all agree with each other which is unusual.. Ta Ta Pet said the reason is that they all think their party will benefit but as they are all in different parties in fact they are agreeing and disagreeing at the same time. I never thought of it like that. I sometimes wonder about Ta Ta Pet. I think he hides his light under a bush. Maybe that's what you have to do when you're an insurance man. In Seaham in county Durham where Ramsay MacDonald is the MP the Labour Party are standing a Mr Shinwell against him.

Sadie was in, she usually comes over when she knows Ta Ta Pet is here because they can chat about shares. He asked her if she had shares in the American First National Bank of Beverley Hills. Sadie asked him, was it a good bank to have shares in and he said, no its gone bust. Well he didn't say it exactly like that but that is what he meant. A lot of film stars have lost a lot of money in it he said. So Sadie said she wasn't sure, she would have to wait till she got in and had a look through her portfolio. That made your dad put his dictionary down. I think a portfolio is a kind of suitcase and the idea of Sadie having a suitcase, never mind a suitcase full of shares is something that you don't think of every day. It creates a strange kind of atmosphere when Sadie starts talking about her shares because we all know she has no money to buy any and Ta Ta Pet won't even know she hasn't got a suitcase to keep them in. We all keep on pretending that she's serious so I think we are all learning something. I know I am and your dad needs to know about shares since he is running the country along with Stan Cole and the others. Ta Ta Pet always treated Sadie respectfully and even more since she said she had three thousand shares in one company.

There's been letters in the Gazette by a farmer's wife and somebody else playing war about men who are trapping wild birds like linnets and skylarks and throstles and keeping them in cages and the poor things are terrified and hurling themselves at the bars of the cage. I wonder how they would like it if somebody put them in cages. It would be a different story then, but some people will do anything for money no matter how cruel it is.

The trade unions have held a congress at Newcastle and they had police guarding them because a lot of unemployed were demonstrating outside. A trade union man from America who was there said there are twelve million unemployed in the USA and sixty three per cent of building workers are out of work. I can't make sense of it. There are lots of people without a house and building workers who would like to build them are out of work. And on top of that you read about rich actors and actresses committing suicide. The husband of the American actress Jean Harlow has shot himself through the head and they'd only been married two months. A British actress living in London has shot herself. Her husband an Army Captain shot himself last month. She's been buried beside him wearing a blue gown her husband gave her and a platinum wedding ring. It's all very romantic and straight out of a woman's magazine, and I feel sorry for her but she was wrong to do that. I wouldn't do that and your dad's out of work so we have hardly any money. I don't think any of the women round here would do that. Some of them would probably be pleased if their ould fella shot himself.

The miners have an international federation. I didn't know that. I thought they just had a trade union, but some of the men who go in Stan Cole's shed were talking about it because the Miners' Federation have had a meeting in London where their President was attacking the communists. He said that they get instructions from Moscow and in Germany instead of attacking the Nazis they were mainly attacking the socialists and dividing the working class. That's not what I read in the papers, it's always the Nazis and the communists fighting each other, but Stan Cole says that the German socialists are not really socialists and the communists are trying to expose them. Anyway this President said that the communists are dividing the workers and this will lead to war in Europe because it will help Hitler and his Nazis get power and they want war. The government in Germany is a minority government, that is it does not have a majority in Parliament and so they have dissolved Parliament and it looks like there will have to be another election which will be the fifth in one year and every election they have the Nazis get stronger.

Mr Walsh has just rode by with his pigeons, lucky man. All he has to think about is his pigeons and will they win a race while I'm just an ignorant housewife surrounded by politicians and trying to work out which one of the bickering lot is right.

Why does that hymn, Nearer my God to Thee come into my head?

I'll have to go, I hear the footsteps of the only non politician in the house coming down our back arch. So tara for now

Your everloving,

Mam

PS We're in mourning. Bolton Wanderers 4 Boro 3. The boro were leading 3 – 1 Bolton were given a penalty. It was a wrong decision, the Bolton Wanderers player fell, he wasn't tripped. I am refusing to draw the curtains but I've told your dad he can wear a black armband if he wants to so long as he doesn't ask me to make it.

Friday 23 September 1932

Dear Bob,

We have received your card telling us that you have now moved to Plymouth. I wonder if that means that you are getting ready to go abroad again. If you are be sure to let us know before you go so that I will not be expecting a card or letter quickly.

Here is some late news just in from the Gazette round our fish and chips. HMS Hood played Middlesbrough at water polo in the new baths. There's a photo in the Gazette of the two teams. The boro won though they don't give the score but I don't think the Hood's team would stand much chance against Middlesbrough with Jack Hatfield playing, there's just nobody to touch him, and the boro are the champions of the North East. The baths are doing very well. Lots of people are going and that's for the old baths as well as the new. We won't be going. It's a shilling to get in the new baths on a Monday night and sixpence every other day. I don't know what's so special about Monday but we can't go to the pictures and the baths though our Jimmy and his pals in Sunnyside go to the old baths every Saturday morning.

When I was at Mrs Levinson's she was playing war about petrol prices going up three pence to one shilling and five pence halfpenny a gallon. She was livid but I thought well we don't have a motor car so it doesn't bother me, then she said that it would affect everything including bus fares. Well I don't use the bus much either, I walk everywhere but if it affects everything while they are cutting the dole and the pancrack that means we are going to be worse off. You don't think of these things, at least I don't or didn't but I will now. Stan Cole hasn't said anything yet but he will, of that we can be sure.

The Government has just come down on Hartlepool for being too generous with the transitional payments, I told you what that is, they are worked out by the public assistance committee but are paid by the Government. They say that the transitional payment should be the same as the poor law relief that the council has to pay. They also say that the public assistance committee have not taken into account the money that some applicants have. There's two cases in the Gazette. One married man had eighty pounds in the bank and the public assistance committee allowed him ten shillings a week. What the Government is saying is that he should not have got anything until he had spent his eighty pounds. And then you think what these Ministers are giving themselves. I'm beginning to sound like Stan Cole. Another married man with two children was allowed twenty seven shillings and sixpence while they were living with his mother who gets six pounds ten shillings a month from her husband who is at sea. This is what the Government calls too generous. I don't know where it is all leading to. There's been awful riots in Birkenhead against the amount of poor relief the public assistance committee pay, with battles with the police, so the public assistance committee has increased the amount they will pay. The Gazette says that if this continues there will be no money to pay any relief at all.

There's a letter in the Gazette from somebody who signs himself Nemo from South Bank. He says that at the meeting of Eston Council last night one of the people who squealed when they were going to reduce teachers salaries voted to cut labourers wages to thirty two shillings a week, that's on top before stoppages. He says what a funny world we live in. Your dad said it is the people at the top in London who are making councillors do this and see how they look after themselves.

Anyway that's enough of me moaning for a bit. I wonder do the other sailors' mothers write letters like this. I sometimes wonder whether I should but then I think you should know what is going on. Ignorance is not bliss, it is just ignorance no matter what some people say.

How's this for a bit of naval history. They are digging foundations for the Tees wharves and a man found what he thought was a marble tablet with words inscribed on it that were in reverse so they could only be read through a mirror. It read HMS Tourmaline. The Tourmaline Galop. Most respectfully dedicated to Mrs Raylton Dixon, and her address and some more words. Anyway a printer said it was not marble it was a kind of limestone used in printing and the words were inscribed on it in reverse so they would come out the right way when it was printed. The stone had been used 57 years ago to print the Tourmaline Galop. She was a steamship with twelve 64 pounder guns. I'll bet your captain doesn't know that.

Stan Cole was on about a man called Ernest Jones who was a leader of the chartist movement a hundred years ago. They were campaigning for some kind of a charter that would give working people the right to vote. Anyway Stan was saying that Mr Jones was a lawyer and his uncle offered to give him £40,000 if he would give up campaigning for the charter and for the rights of the poor. He wouldn't so his uncle left the money to his gardener. He was also offered a job as a judge if he would give up and he refused. Stan said compare that with politicians today. Anyway this story is being told now because Mr Jones's daughter is now old and going blind and living in poverty and she has had to pawn all her things. So I said to Stan how do you know and he said he had just read it. The old lady is living on the south coast at a place called Leigh on sea. I think that is very sad, that a man who could have been very rich and his daughter living like that. I wonder what he would have done if he could have known. Sacrificing your self is one thing but sacrificing your family is another. You would think these Labour party politicians would help her.

That Russian who assassinated the French President has been sent to the guillotine. I know it was awful what he did but the poor man had to be dragged out of the prison by two warders holding him up to the guillotine. They did it in public in front of a crowd who came to watch. Just the thought of it makes my blood run cold.

Did you see the eclipse the other night? It was very impressive.

Councillor Eckert has been speaking in Middlesbrough about his visit to New York. The Mayor of New York has resigned because people say he was involved in something shady and the man who is acting as mayor gave Councillor Eckert an introduction card to get him to see people. He says that prohibition is not working. There are hundreds of speakeasies, you can even buy drinks in theatres and he saw lots of drunken men on the streets and the gangsters are just like you see at the pictures. He was coming out of a restaurant when he saw two men with guns holding up the cash desk. A detective arrived and ordered them to put their hands up. They didn't so he shot one dead and the other escaped. He said everybody is talking about the kidnapping of the Lindbergh baby. He said there are over a million men, women and children dependent on charity and there are long queues at Salvation Army citadels and churches waiting for bread and coffee. I'm glad we don't live in America.

Sadie was in and she asks to be remembered. She didn't talk about shares for a change. I suppose with just me in she wouldn't think it was worth it but she was telling me about two boys who made money at Stockton carnival selling raffle tickets, tuppence each, for two ducks and the winner got two plastic ducks worth a penny each. I want to laugh but it's no laughing matter cheating people like that. On that note I will say Tara for now. The jam and bread kid has just walked in. He wants to be remembered.

Your everloving,
Mam
PS Boro 0 Liverpool 1

Friday 30 September 1932

Dear Bob,

How are you. We are wondering where you are now but we will have to be patient. The more I learn about the history of Middlesbrough the more fascinated I get. The Tees-side Golf Club has just got a new headquarters which used to be the Mandale Granary and was on the bank of the Tees. Ships used to call there. When the river was straightened out starting in 1825 the Mandale Granary was no longer on the bank. They reckon it was opposite a pub called The Anchor Inn which would have been on Acklam Road. That's as much as I know about golf except that our Jimmy and the other boys go up to the golf course looking for lost golf balls. Jimmy was telling me about one of the tricks that a boy out of Laurel Avenue gets up to. You know if you go up Woodville Avenue to the three cornered wood where the golf course is. Follow the golf course across Saltersgill lane and you come to a bend in the beck. Well the golf balls sometimes land in the beck or close to it. This boy is hiding beneath the bank of the beck and if a ball lands near he creeps out and gets the ball and sinks it in the sand a the bottom of the beck. Or if they land in the beck he does the same. That's really stealing and I told our Jimmy he better not do that. The tricks they get up to. You can't imagine it.

Mrs Nelson who lives across the road but a bit further down told me she has started keeping a scrap book and she sticks all the advertisements in it so she can compare them to see which will do her the most good and she will save them for her grandchildren so they can see what goes on. She sticks them in with a dab of condensed milk so it's more than the adverts that they will be getting. I said that, not Mrs Nelson. Anyway her latest is for bile beans. A man in Diamond Road says his food wasn't doing him a scrap of good, it lay undigested just like a leaden weight in his inside. His stomach was in such a bad way that for months at a time he lived on milk and biscuits. After two boxes of bile beans his problem was solved. Now he takes them every night. The adverts say that the bile beans are worth a guinea a box so he must be worth a bit by now. Mrs Nelson brought her scrap book into Sadie's while there was a gang of us there and we were wondering what sort of biscuits he was eating. That isn't all that we were wondering.

Talking about food Mr Gandhi in India just finished fasting in prison. I don't know why he's in prison but he went on fast because the Government was going to bring in new election laws which would separate people into what they call Hindus and the depressed which I am told means the untouchables. He said that he did not want anybody else to go on fast but they should set about doing what they can to remove what he calls untouchability. Don't ask me to explain this because I can't but the representatives of both sides went to see Gandhi because they don't want this electoral system. Anyway he finished his fast because the high caste Indians and the untouchables have reached an agreement and the Government has accepted it. In Bengal somebody was putting a leaflet out telling everyone to slaughter all Europeans but the papers say that the Indians have a legislative assembly, which is like our Parliament, and they called these people terrorists. The Indian MPs said they would help the Government to beat the terrorists because if they won and Britain left the Indian people wouldn't have democracy they would have government by guns and bombs and the Indian Ministers would have to do what the terrorists told them to do.

The Germans are at it again. One of their leading lights has demanded the return of their colonies that they lost in the war. He is saying that it is a lie that the Germans were responsible for the war and the Treaty of Versailles should be scrapped and instead of spending money on feeding the unemployed Germans should settle in Africa and develop it. Hitler and his Nazi party are saying the same thing. It sounds silly to me because look how many men are out of work here and if having colonies gets rid of unemployment how is it we have colonies and unemployment. In fact things are getting worse. There's a man got a letter in the Gazette who's done his homework. He says that two months ago the public assistance committee promised to increase relief. At that time he was getting twelve shillings and sixpence a week. Now he gets five shillings and five shillings worth of goods. He's written down the price of food showing how much it has risen in price and shows that what he is getting is really worth only eight shillings and eleven pence not the fifteen shillings and three pence the public assistance committee had promised him. The editor of the Gazette has written about a living wage and says that the pinch of poverty is being felt in high places. The Governor of the Bank of England only gets two thousand pounds a year and the other directors get less than that. So the Court of the Bank of England, whoever they are, have decided to double their salaries. Just think of that. Even with my simple arithmetic I work that out at about eighty pounds a week. To be fair the editor says that if they can increase their own salaries they should increase everybody else's and that would let people buy more and would create jobs. But eighty pounds a week. I can't even dream about having that much.

There's been blood on the moon in Middlesbrough's council chamber. Some of the councillors are saying that the Government should come and do their own dirty work administering the means test. Twenty men from here have joined the hunger march to London against the means test and the cuts in the dole and there's an argument about whether they should get public assistance because they are not available for work. There's a man been in court for absconding from Holgate, that's the posh name for the workhouse wearing one of their suits. Anyway the police got him and in court he was charged with deserting from Holgate wearing clothes valued at two pounds ten shillings. So he opened his jacket and said two pounds ten shillings, I wouldn't give you six bob for the lot. So the clerk of the court said alright we'll say valued at six shillings. So he said you wouldn't get five shillings so the clerk said alright we'll say five shillings and then he was given fourteen days in prison. He had sixteen previous convictions so I suppose he can't complain.

I think I told you that the Middlesbrough Labour Party has split much to the delight of Stan Cole, your granddad and Mrs Levinson. Well some of them have now formed a new party, the Middlesbrough socialist party. I asked Stan Cole if he would be joining but he just scoffed. He says they are not real socialists like him.

Well Bob, I'll have to go. School's out and the jam and bread kid will be arriving any minute. Don't forget to write or send us a post card. I'm collecting them. Tara for now. Everybody asks to be remembered.

Your ever loving
Mam

PS Leicester 1 Boro 1. I have to tell you that Camsell collided with their goalkeeper and he was all shook up for the rest of the match. Camsell, not the goal keeper. And I have to tell you that Hinton's porridge oats are three pence a pound. I don't know why your dad wants me to tell you that. Is this some secret code you've both got worked out?

PPS He's just thought on. Max Schmeling beat Nicky Walker in New York. Walker's manager wouldn't let him come out of his corner for the ninth round he was in such a bad way. So Schmeling might be fighting Jack Sharkey for the world heavy weight title.

Friday 7 October 1932

Dear Bob,

Just to let you know we have received your card from Gibraltar and to say we are pleased to hear that you are well and wondering when we will see you again.

There are lots of people writing in the Gazette about the people of Nile Street being given houses in the Ayresome ward and some of the people who live in Nile Street are really angry about being told that they would not be suitable tenants.

There's lots of big meetings going on here. The Labour Party had a big open air meeting in Billingham with Margaret Bondfield who is one of the top Labour Party people speaking. There were two thousand people there. She said the way to solve unemployment is to increase wages and work shorter hours. Mrs Levinson put the tin hat on that when I was round there to do the cleaning. She said that would put more people out of work because it would make our goods more expensive and our exports would fall. So I said well why don't we just sell them in Britain and she said that because the prices would have gone up they would be cheaper to buy from other countries and so we would import them and that would put our workers out of work. Then she said that we would have a deficit on our balance of payments so I said what is the balance of payments. She said that we trade with other countries, they buy from us and we sell to them. If we are buying more from them than they are buying from us then they have lots of English pounds that they can't use so they ask the Bank of England to change them into gold or a currency that they want like say American dollars. That means the Bank of England's reserves of gold and foreign currency go down and we face an economic crisis because the day will come when we can't change the pounds into gold or another currency so people abroad will not want pounds at all. So I said what will the Government do then and she said increase interest rates so that foreigners will lend us money which will go into the reserves. But it will also make it more expensive to buy things on the never never and so we will buy less from other countries. At the same time it will be more expensive for British manufacturers to borrow to buy new machinery and raw materials to make things and so we will have more unemployment. I would never have remembered all this so Mrs Levinson wrote it all down while I got on with the cleaning, so I could show it to your dad. With him being the chancellor of the exchequer in Stan Cole's shed, Mrs Levinson doesn't know that, I thought it might help him. It's only confused me and it will come as news to him. In Stan Cole's shed it's dead simple, get rid of the capitalists and everything will be fine. Mrs Levinson is beginning to convince me that it won't and I think that is why she is telling me all this. She's really cute the way she does it.

Some of us were standing gassing at Sadie's front gate, I don't know why we say her front gate because she hasn't got a back one. Anyway we were standing there when along comes Mrs Turner on her way home from the bottom shops and she said Dracula is in Meadowfield and it looks like he's coming this way. Well Mrs Callaghan shot off to let their Gyp out and she came back with him and he was waging his tail and we were all saying good dog. Then Mr Muir came along and started on about Mr de Valera. Ever since he learnt that Mr de Valera is a chief of an Indian tribe and is called Eagle Dressing His Feathers he goes on about him. Well it seems he's in London to meet the Government, Eagle Dressing His Feathers, not Mr Muir, and he's not agreeing to anything. Well that was getting Sadie going because she can't stand de Valera and she was just getting into her stride when Dracula came riding into Sunnyside. Well as soon as Gyp saw him he was at him and he barked at his left foot all the way up Sunnyside and out of sight round the corner into the Vale. Then Gyp came trotting back looking very pleased with himself. Mrs Callaghan gave him a biscuit out of her pinny and we all congratulated him.

The Liberals had a big meeting in the Town Hall last night. It was packed to hear the leader Sir Herbert Samuel and the two Middlesbrough Liberal MPs Kingsley Griffiths and Ernest Young. Mr Samuel said the Liberals had left the National Government because they did not agree with what the Government had agreed to at Ottawa where they were meeting the governments of the Dominions. He said the Ottawa Agreement would mean taxes on food and they had promised the electors that they would not support that. He also said that with Imperial Preference we are limiting our trade to twenty two million people who live in the Dominions when we should be trading with the rest of the world's one thousand five hundred millions. Your granddad was at the meeting so he told me all this. He's a liberal so he agreed with Mr Samuel. When I was round at Mrs Levinson's she disagreed with what he said and said it was all rubbish. The other countries have trade barriers against us and that is why we need protection. Stan Cole said it is all the fault of capitalism and the workers have to unite to get rid of the capitalists. Your dad agreed with Stan Cole. Ta Ta Pet said on the one hand this and on the other hand that and Sadie wanted to know how it would affect share prices. So there it is, clear as mud. I think I'm with Ta Ta Pet. It's only a pity I've only got two hands. . .

Whatever about that, the capitalists Dorman Longs have got a contract to build a bridge in Denmark. It's going to be over two miles long made of British steel going over a stretch of water at a place called Stormstrommen and it will be high enough to let ships under it. So there's some work coming to Middlesbrough.

The people who left the Labour Party in Middlesbrough and formed the Middlesbrough Socialist Party have had a meeting in the Co-op hall. They say they have 160 members and they are going to provide political education to teach people about socialism and they are going to get socialists elected to the

Town council. Mr Harford is going to be their candidate in Vulcan Ward. I said to Stan Cole that they will be putting his shed out of business but he wouldn't bite.

Well Bob that's all this time Everybody asks to be remembered. I'll have to go, jam and bread time is looming.

We are going to the Hippodrome to see All Quiet on the Western Front. Your dad said he has heard it is very good and it is an anti-war film. Tara for now.

Your everloving,

Mam

PS Boro 5 Portsmouth 4

Friday 14 October 1932

Dear Bob,

Here I am again with me acid drops. How are you. We all think of you and wonder where you are now. Gibraltar was the last we heard of you. I wonder if you are going into the Mediterranean.

Our Jimmy keeps pestering me for a yo yo. Woolworths had a yo yo competition last week for boys and girls up to 15. Jimmy doesn't have a yo yo but as a result of the competition he is pestering me to get him one. Woolworths are not daft, they knew that their competition would make more children want a yo yo.

Mrs Nelson is a knockout. I think I told you she has started to cut advertisements out of the paper and stick them in a scrapbook. She read one out for Dr Cassell's tablets.

Dr Cassell Tablets one shilling and three pence a bottle. Mrs Manley of Romford was rescued from years of misery in one short month. I asked her to tell me the story of her sufferings. "I suffered" she said "from pains all over my body, in my head, limbs and often my stomach. I don't know how I stood it. The pains were often sharp and lasting, so that I used to cry out with the very agony of them."

"You tried everything of course" I asked

"Yes but I never got any relief at all until I tried Dr Cassell tablets."

"And they cured you in a month."

"Yes. In one month the trouble vanished completely."

Mrs Nelson read it out then she said she suffered pain like that for years as well. So she bought some tablets. She said she's been giving them to her old man crushed up in his tea for two months and he still hasn't vanished. It's the way she tells it dead straight faced, not a sign of a crack.

I can recommend fish and chips wrapped up in old Gazettes for keeping you up to date with the news. I was on my knees lighting the fire and reading the paper as usual before I put it in the fireplace and there was a piece about America. It said there are two hundred thousand homeless boys wandering about in America. There are some girls as well. These boys are hopping on freight trains and traveling from town to town. The railroads try to keep them off but towns have such problems with relief that they give the children twenty four hours to move on. They have a children's Bureau and they say these children are a potential social menace. You can see how they will be. They have to eat and if they have to steal they will and then they will be on the way to being criminals. I just wonder how parents can let their children go like that.

It's the time for the Irish sweepstake again but I am not going to have a share in a ticket this time. I don't see why I should help that man de Valera and anyway I haven't any money so I'm killing two birds with one stone. There's a big argument going on here about whether we should have a sweepstake to pay for British hospitals instead of for Irish hospitals. Some people are opposed because they say it would be immoral, it would be encouraging people to gamble. Work that one out.

There's a man lives in Cambridge Road so he must know what he is talking about has a letter in the Gazette saying he was at the big Liberal meeting in the Town Hall, the one your granddad was at, and he said the speakers had nothing for traders and the unemployed, just for the banks, nobody must touch them. Well I don't know how anybody could touch a bank apart from walking past and trailing your hand along the wall. But if you live in Cambridge Road you're not daft so I think it's like your dad once said, politicians say one thing and the audience hear something else. It's like that old saying, "he always gets Hobs for Jones". You say Jones and he hears Hobs. I'm like that with Stan Cole sometimes, he says one thing and I hear another. But I think that's Stan's fault for not being clear.

The Labour Party have been having a national conference and they have decided to abolish the House of Lords, nationalise the mines, support free trade and have nothing to do with the Labour Party leaders who joined the National Government. Well I don't mind them abolishing the House of

Lords, what do they do for us, and nationalising the mines. The wages there are less than thirty shillings a week and you see the miners risking their lives digging the coal out and the Lords in their mansions sitting there doing nothing and getting paid because they say the coal under their big estates belongs to them. I was reading that the coal was formed thousands of years ago by dying forests so how could it belong to them. But free trade, I don't know about that, letting foreigners dump their steel here while our steelworks are closed doesn't seem like a good idea.

The Conservatives have had a conference as well though they were at Blackpool and the Labour Party were at Leicester. Mr Levinson went and he told Mrs Levinson about it and she was telling me all about it so it was get the ginger biscuits out with the tea. I know when she says get the ginger biscuits out I'm in for it. It wouldn't be so bad if I got the lecture instead of doing the cleaning but I get the lecture and do the cleaning. She's not bad though and I don't know what we would do without the money. I think I'm what they call a captive audience. Anyway the Chancellor of the Exchequer Neville Chamberlain was speaking there and he said that the Government had converted a large part of the national debt into lower interest rate Treasury bonds and that is saving the country a lot of money and now he was setting up a committee to tell him how to cut local council spending. The money saved could be used to cut taxes and that would be good for the economy. That's not the way Stan Cole sees it but when he is in our house he has to be polite and not swear so I knew that when he was saying Hobs he was thinking Jones

There's been terrible riots in Belfast looting and setting fire to places and the police patrolling the streets in steel cages to protect them and using their guns. It's strange now I come to think of it, our bobbies don't carry guns but in Belfast they do. I can't imagine PC Masterman carrying a gun. He just pushes his bike and sometimes he gets on it. In Belfast there are streets barricaded and there is a ten o'clock curfew. The police are blaming the communists but it is all about outdoor relief for the unemployed. The trade unions are meeting the Lord Mayor of Belfast to ask him to get the Board of Guardians to pay the same rates of relief as they pay in England. If they get less than us then they must be desperate. A Communist in Stockton called George Short has been meeting the Board of Guardians there to ask them not to be harsh on the men marching to London on the hunger march. He wants them to give relief to their families while they are away and unavailable for work. If this is what the people of Belfast want may God help them.

Well Bob, on that sad note I must leave you. Oh I nearly forgot. Sylvia is coming round on Sunday to get her hair done. She particularly asks me to remember her to you. That goes for all of us here. Tara for now. Guess who's just walked in starving.

Your everloving,

Mam

PS Chelsea 2 Boro 1

Friday 21 October 1932

Dear Bob,

How are you? Are you sunning yourself somewhere? The last we heard you were in Gibraltar. Sylvia was telling me that she had a letter from you saying that you were in Gibraltar but nothing since.

You know I like to keep you up to date with letters from readers in the Gazette. Well here's one I have copied out for you. There's some kind of battle going on in Saltburn because the Gazette headline is A Duel in Saltburn and I really enjoyed reading this letter. I only wish I could write like it. I copy these letters out so that maybe by doing that some of it will rub off on me. It's a kind of way of getting an education really. Anyway this letter is from a man who signs himself Business First. Saltburn.

Dear Sir, According to a report in the Gazette some days ago, a meeting of the Saltburn Ratepayers Association is to be held tomorrow night. With that modesty which is his distinguishing characteristic Mr F.W.Sibley asked the public to lend him their ears, for he is to use the occasion of the meeting to reply to Councillor H.W.Pilkington. The implication was that the retort was to be crushing and full of the Sibley brand of coruscating wit and irony. The speech to which Mr Sibley is to reply occupied two and a quarter hours. Nobody doubts Mr Sibley's capability to equal or even surpass Mr Pilkington's feat. But the question is, who wants to hear him? Or even more pertinently still, who if they intend to hear him, really believes that the address will advance the cause of public progress and welfare by the slightest jot or tittle. Signed Business First Saltburn

You get some great letters in the Gazette. Some of the words I don't really understand but you get the meaning. While your dad was out I took a sneaky look in his dictionary. He still doesn't like anybody else to touch it. He even dusts it himself, not that it needs a lot of dusting the time he spends reading it. Anyway I looked up coruscating. It seemed like the kind of word that I might find useful, just to throw it in to the conversation now and again. It means to sparkle or to throw off flashes of light. Well I can do that. I've been coruscating all over the place for years without knowing it. The other word was irony. I don't really understand what it means it's so complicated. The dictionary says conveyance of meaning by words whose literal meaning is the opposite. Well I don't know what literal means so I was going to look up literal when I heard your dad coming round the back so I had to get his dictionary back on the shelf before he walked in. When he did I did a bit of coruscating. He just asked me if I was alright. He meant in the head. I think all those flashing lights must have been getting in his eyes.

There's still a big argument going on in the Town Council about the means test. The Public Assistance Committee want to refuse to run the means test the way the Government wants them to. But the Council had to agree to that and they didn't. They said that if Middlesbrough Council refuse to run the means test the way the Government wants them to then the Government will run it for them. So they are between the devil and the deep blue sea. Councillor Carey who is on the public assistance committee said Middlesbrough was saving the Government a hundred thousands pounds a year and still the Government wasn't satisfied. Councillor Meehan said that if the Council rejected the means test that would help the revolt throughout the country. That worries me because it seems like a good idea at the time but we have seen the riots in Belfast and Birkenhead and how the Government reacted to them and we don't want that here. Councillor Cooper said 1932 would go down in history as the year two great things were born, the means test and the yo yo. I think he was trying to be funny but there's nothing funny about the means test.

The Gazette has been having a go at the Labour Party leader Mr Lansbury. He has written a letter to the Times saying there are now nearly three million unemployed and the last twelve years for the unemployed have been years of degradation, starvation and destitution. The Gazette says that he should not forget that there were two Labour Governments in that time. Stan Cole's reply to that was that the Labour Government in 1924 lasted nine months and the one in 1929 lasted two years and they never had a majority in Parliament so you can't really count that as Labour Government. The Gazette says the problem is world wide and the Ottawa Agreements will lead to increased trade and we are trying to get agreement to reduce armaments. I read the paper and I listen to the arguments by Stan, your dad, your granddad, Mrs Levinson and it's like a maze. I end up knowing no more than when I started out. I keep telling myself that I am not going to listen anymore but there's no escape. Then just when I think I've had as much as I can stand Sadie comes in and starts talking about shares. She was in talking to Ta Ta Pet. She wanted his advice on whether she should buy some new gilt edged Government securities or some shares in a paper company. She brought in a crumpled up piece of the Gazette which had obviously been round their fish and chips to read from. So they were straightening it out on our table and Ta Ta Pet took a look at it and he said she should buy the shares in the paper company. He said the Government gilt edged would give her two per cent, that is two pounds on every hundred pounds she invested and he asked her how many thousands she was thinking of investing. Sadie said she hadn't made her mind up yet which had me and your dad in stitches. Jimmy was surprised because he said have you got thousands of pounds. Sadie is going to regret saying that. It will be round Sunnyside in no time. Anyway Ta Ta Pet was reading the paper and he said that if she bought the paper shares she would get six per cent and if the price of the shares rose on the stock exchange she could sell and make a profit. So he asked her if she was feeling bullish or bearish but she said she was feeling stony broke and it didn't look as if things were going to get any better so she supposed she was feeling bearish. I think I told you that a bull is somebody who thinks share prices will rise and the bear thinks they will fall. How those two keep their faces straight I'll never know.

Sadie was telling me that she has heard from her sister Pat in Canada. Sadie hadn't heard from her in a long time because she has been moving around and Sadie never had an address to write to. Anyway she has written to say she is in Halifax in Canada but she hasn't given an address because she may be moving and she will write again.

The Gazette has been having a go at the Government over trade with Russia. The Gazette says there is a lot of trade to be done with the Russians because they are building up industry at a very fast pace and they are rapidly becoming a modern industrial nation. They have built a big dam across the river

Dniepner and are turning uneducated peasants into skilled workers. and we are losing opportunities to export steel and machinery to them. We have sent twenty thousand tons of steel this year from Teesside but the Russians need credit to buy more and the Government is refusing. Yet Germany is giving credits and have doubled their exports to Russia. I hope the Government will listen to the Gazette because it could mean a lot of work round here.

Well Bob, I'm going on a bit as per usual. The jam and bread kid will be arriving shortly so I better go. Everybody asks to be remembered. Tara for now.

Your everloving
Mam

PS Nostradamus sitting in the corner there has taken his nose out of his dictionary to say Boro 1 Huddersfield 1

Friday 28 October 1932

Dear Bob,

How are you? My usual question I know but I find it difficult to think of different ways of starting. Ta Ta Pet has been telling me about the examinations you have to pass in the Navy to get promotion. He read it in the paper somewhere but I must have missed it. Mathematics, geography, history, seamanship and general knowledge. Ta Ta Pet said they gave examples of questions that are asked in general knowledge. Names of national politicians in other countries as well as our own, reparations, payment of war debts, exchange rates, names of plants, I don't know what they want that for, and astronomy. When I think of all the things that I have told you in my letters, not sums, or geography or history except the history of Middlesbrough or plants or stars, but everything else you should pass with flying colours. I will definitely keep on telling you these things now I know that.

Mrs Rawlins has just gone past with two shopping bags nearly pulling her arms out of their sockets. It will be apples and sugar for toffee apples and toffee umbrellas. Mrs Callender has just gone by in her fox fur. She's probably going to Mrs Turnbull's for a glass of her rhubarb wine and a natter. Mr Walsh has rode past with his pigeons on the front of his bike. I mean they are in a box not perched on his handlebars. The coal man's just been, so Sunnyside is having a busy day.

We just need Dracula to ride past with Gyp on his heels and the day will be complete.

Ta Ta Pet and Sadie were in. She always comes across when she knows he's here so she can chat with him about her shares which she likes to crack on about but hasn't got. Anyway she got on about the Rector of Stiffkey, you know the one I told you about who got the sack. Well she knew I'd been taking an interest in it and she came over with the Gazette that she got round their fish and chips. It said that their reporter had been to see the rectory where the Rector, his name is Davidson had lived for a long time. Well Sadie read out what he wrote. "Today the fine old Rectory where Mr Davidson had lived for so long stood deserted among its neglected gardens and thickly clustered trees. When our reporter knocked on the door the noise echoed away as through an empty house and there was no response, although there are still curtains at the window and some of Mr Davidson's pictures can be seen hanging on the walls."

Well you should have seen the effect on Ta Ta Pet. Straightaway he stood up and started spouting poetry. Is there anybody there, Said the traveller, Knocking on the moonlit door, And his horse in the silence champed the grasses, Of the forest's ferny floor.

And he went on and on. This is the second time he's done this and he doesn't take his bicycle clips off. People don't expect him to take his bicycle clips off when he's just marking the insurance book but reciting poetry is not like marking an insurance book. He just stood there in the middle of our mat in his bicycle clips with his arm pointing at the ceiling, Is there anybody there said the traveller. Well I know we were all here but when he'd gone your dad wondered if he was all there. Ta Ta Pet, not your dad. Mind you it was a nice poem. I asked him to write it out for me and he said he will bring it next week. It's by a man called Walter de la Mare. I think Ta Ta Pet recites poetry like that because he's so cultured. It wouldn't surprise me if he was sitting at home reading poetry when your dad's in the Cleveland singing Nellie Dean.

I've been reading about the origins of Middlesbrough's street names. It owes a lot to the Quakers who founded our town. On the other side of the railway where the original town hall is the streets were named North, South, East and West. Then we got Stockton Street, Cleveland Street, Durham Street and Linthorpe Lane. After the Duke of Sussex visited the town Linthorpe Lane was changed to Sussex Street. Then as the town expanded streets were named after members of the aristocracy like Suffield Street, Russell Street, Feversham Street. The town honoured the Dundas family. Then when Queen Victoria came to the throne we got Queen's Square, that's over the other side of the railway, just under the bridge, and when she married Prince Albert streets were named Albert Road, Victoria Street I don't know where that is unless it was changed to Victoria Road. Our railway station is the second one, I think the first one must have been at Newport.. But when the station was built we got Station Street and at the corner of that there was the Station Hotel where Mr Gladstone made a speech in 1852 in which he said that Middlesbrough was the youngest child of England's enterprise. After that they named streets after the iron masters like Bolckow and Vaughan and Fidler. Then when the borough fields were built on they used the names of trees like Laurel Street and Maple Street. I know that they used to call the area this side of the Town Hall the dark continent. I can't imagine why. Cannon Street got its name from the cannon that used to stand where St Columba's church is now. Local artillery men used to practise on it. How's this for a laugh, Mary Ann Street was named after the builder's daughter Mary Ann Sharp. So now I know where streets got their names from. Maybe one day they will name one after Stan Cole. They could call it Shed Street, and how about Ta Ta Pet Street? They could have a pub at every corner of that one with people saying Ta Ta at chucking out time.

Your dad and me were standing at our gate when Mr Wells came walking by. He's an engine driver and a big man in the railwaymen's union. He was telling your dad that the bosses on the railways want to reduce railwaymen's wages again to thirty eight shillings a week. They've already got trouble with transferring men to other districts then expecting the men to pay their own lodgings and keep their families at home. There's no limit to what they will do if they can get away with it. There's a miners strike at Ryhope Colliery in County Durham and a crowd of women attacked six miners who were going to work even though there was a strike. They call them blacklegs. The police had to rescue them.

It was lecture time at Mrs Levinson's this week so it was out with the tea and ginger biscuits. This week it was the Ottawa Agreements and steel tariffs. She said that when import duties were first put on steel it was only for three months so the other countries kept on dumping their steel in Britain but the Ottawa Agreements made them permanent and that is good for our steel industry. The Government has said that in return for them putting duties on imports of steel the steel companies have to modernise.

There's a man, Mr Wall, got a letter in the Gazette saying that the way to end unemployment is to bring in Prohibition. He says that he wrote to the Gazette a year ago before the present financial crisis and if the Government had taken notice of him they would have saved £200 million a year and would not have had to cut services. At the same time I've read that if the American Government legalised booze they would collect 754 million dollars in tax. They have prohibition and millions out of work. I wonder if Mr Wall read that.

Another letter says the city fathers have put the old black maria into Stewarts Park and now it is known as the Black Maria Ice Cream Bar. It's signed Pie Can. The letter not the black maria. This is the man who wrote some time ago when somebody complained that he had to pay sixpence for a pork pie with a crest on it in Stewarts Park and he could have got one without the crest for two pence in the town. Pie Can said that man did not understand the value of first issues and if he hung on to it it could be valuable.

Well Bob, I think that's enough for this time. I will write again next week and keep you up to date with what's going on here. Everybody asks to be remembered. I was talking to Sylvia in the Stores and she said she had written. I better get the jam and bread out so I'm ready. It's sort of first aid.
Tara for now.
Your everloving
Mam
PS Sunderland 2 Boro 1

Friday 4 November 1932

Dear Bob,

We've received your letter saying that you are in Bermuda again and Sylvia has heard from you as well so it is good to know that you are in good health and spirits although I wonder when we are going to see you again.

Life goes on pretty much the same here, always hoping that things will pick up and your dad can get a job again. The Tees Conservancy Commissioners are dredging the river and using the soil to reclaim land on the North bank to build factories on so somebody must know something or else why would they be doing that. The Commissioners have done a lot over the years straightening the river and widening it and they built the breakwater. There's an article in the Gazette about it saying that it took 24 years to complete. Men go down there fishing now with rods catching whiting and mackerel. Cotton workers have gone on strike and there's been a hunger march to London. Some men went from here and there was a demonstration in Hyde Park. Sadie's sister Kathleen was telling us about Hyde Park and Marble Arch when she was here and I remembered that there is a big hotel at Marble Arch that was built with steel girders from Middlesbrough. I would like to see it but I don't suppose I ever will. There was a riot in Hyde Park but the police say that the hunger marchers were not responsible. The police saw cudgels with nails sticking out being unloaded from a van. It's terrible that those men and women marched all that way then somebody does a thing like that. Then there was more trouble in Trafalgar Square so the police raided the hunger marchers headquarters in London and arrested a man called Wal Hannington who is a communist and the leader of the hunger marchers movement and he's been charged with incitement to mutiny. It's surprising what is going on behind the scenes that you don't know about. A man from Durham Street in Middlesbrough, a Mr Brennan was arrested. He has been accused of throwing a half brick at a police inspector and being in possession of another piece of brick. When he was searched he had nine copies of the Daily Worker in his pocket. Stan Cole reads the Daily Worker, but fancy that man going all the way to London to throw bricks at policemen and getting the hunger marchers a bad name.

There's a man been caught cheating when he was claiming off the Public Assistance and he's been sent to prison for dole fraud. He told the investigating officer that the only money coming into the house was his mother's widow's pension of ten shillings a week and nine shillings that his sister earned so he was given the maximum transitional benefit of fifteen shillings and three pence a week. Then they found out that his mother was renting three houses as well as the one they lived in and she was letting the houses out in rooms and from the three houses she was making a profit of thirty five shillings a week. That is wicked. No wonder the government says we have to have a means test and it's the honest ones that suffer.

Mrs Nelson was in Sadie's reading one of the advertisements she keeps in her adverts scrap book. Yeast Vite.

When pain tortures you, when Weakness and Weariness overtake you, when frayed and shattered nerves conspire to make your life a martyrdom, a tablet or two of Yeast Vite will bring quick relief. 5-30 minutes.
"Can't work old chap? Buck up old man. Take some Yeast Vite tablets – they banished my nervousness in 20 minutes yesterday. They'll make you feel like doing two days work in one"

So then we were all having a hilarious time thinking about who would benefit from a dose. I told Stan Cole about it just to get his reaction. He said he would become nervous if he felt like doing two days work in one and would go to the doctors for a check up. He said if any tablets made fellas feel like doing two days work in one the bosses would be handing them out free when they clocked on.

We went to the Gaumont to see Tarzan and the Apes. I'd read Edgar Rice Burrough's book out of the library so I wanted to see the picture. Johnny Weismuller the world champion swimmer was Tarzan. They say he has the finest physique of any living man but they haven't seen your dad's. It's about an Englishman who lives in the jungle among the apes and can't speak English so your dad could have played that role. Then I could have been Jane teaching him. Anyway enough of that, some English people are walking through the jungle looking for a secret valley where elephants are supposed to go to die. The explorers want to make a fortune out of the ivory. Their leader has taken his daughter Maureen O'Hara, that could have been me sez me patting me hair, with them and Tarzan kidnaps her and they live together swinging through the trees. She has to teach him to speak so they start off with me Tarzan you Jane. I enjoyed it, being Jane I mean.

Jock Muir and Taffy Evans came down the street when Sadie and me were talking at our gate. Straightaway Jock got on about Mr de Valera or Eagle Dressing his Feathers as he always calls him now and Taff asked him what he meant because he didn't know. So Jock told him and he spun it out so he could enjoy it all the more. I think he's having a sly dig at Sadie because he knows that she doesn't like de Valera but at the same time she doesn't like hearing him called by that name. Anyway Jock then went on about de Valera demanding £400 million from the British Government for taxes that the British Government had collected in Ireland. We all agreed that he could whistle for it so at least we were in agreement about something. When Sadie's sister Kathleen was here I asked her why Sadie hates Mr de Valera so much and she said it was because some of their relatives were killed in the Easter rising in Dublin in 1916 and they didn't even have anything to do with it. I know that Sadie thinks Ireland should be in with England, Scotland and Wales and shouldn't be separate. Talking about Ireland the statue of Mr Bolckow opposite the General Post Office where the bus exchange is now, was unveiled by Lord Cavendish at Middlesbrough's Jubilee. Then he went to Ireland and was murdered in Phoenix Park by some Irishmen who stabbed him to death. Then they were caught and executed. Isn't that an awful useless waste of people's lives.

Mrs Levinson was telling me that Mussolini who is the fascist dictator of Italy has said that all Europe will be fascist in ten years and we have to arm to stop him and Hitler because things are looking bad in Germany and Mussolini must know something to say that, he wouldn't just be guessing. I said if Mussolini and Hitler are that bad why do people vote for them and she said because they make promises to get people back into work and people are desperate and they say we have tried the other parties so let's give the fascists a chance and if they do then they will not be able to get the fascists out again. She said the communists are the same, look at Russia.

Well Bob, I'll have to go. Jimmy came in a few minutes ago, saw me writing and collapsed starving on the mat. Only a slice of jam and bread will revive him. So tara for now. Everybody asks to be remembered.

Your everloving,
Mam

PS Your dad was sitting in his corner reading his dictionary and I was going to say you Tarzan me Jane then I thought I better not, he might start swinging on the electric light so I didn't say anything. Anyway Tarzan's gone out to Stan Cole's shed and left a message with Jane, Birmingham 1 Boro 4 .Two goals by Camsell were not allowed

Friday 11 November 1932

Dear Bob,

We have received your letter saying that you are at Ireland Island Bermuda and Sadie was interested wondering where it got its name from. Anyway you will be having warmer weather than us and I hope you are enjoying it.

The other day was an enjoyable day for me, I beat Mrs Smithers to the horse muck. I heard the coalman so I went out and while I was standing at our gate his horse obliged. Well I rushed into our house and grabbed my bucket and shovel and was standing at the back of the cart waiting for it to move when Mrs Smithers arrived with her bucket. Well I was there first and I was first in the queue when the cart moved. I've never enjoyed shoveling horse muck so much in my life. I made the most of it and when I straightened up I pretended my back was aching and I started talking to her about how bending down to shovel horse muck can make your back ache. Then I watched her going home with an empty bucket. I was singing all day. What made it so good is that its not often that I get there first. I'm sure Mrs Smithers could break the record for the hundred yards sprint wearing her pinny and carrying her bucket and shovel. Her little legs just twinkle down Sunnyside. There was nobody in the house and I was feeling so pleased with myself that I sat in the armchair with my feet up and to give myself a little treat I had a read of your dad's dictionary. He'll never know the pleasure that brought me.

I was reading that a young boxer collapsed in his dressing room after a boxing match and died in hospital. He was only 24. It seems such a waste and his family must be feeling terrible. I don't know what the other boxer must be feeling like. I don't know what can be done about it, boys want to box and for many of them it is a way out of poverty they hope.

Dracula's just rode past on his sit up and beg. I can't hear Gyp so it looks like he's going to be lucky this time. Stockton Board of Guardians met a delegation from the unemployed workers who were asking for an extra five shillings a week for eight weeks before and after Christmas, a bag of coal a week, food centres and boots for children of the unemployed. Mr George Short told them that if they did not help the unemployed there would be riots like in Birkenhead. I don't know how he knows that. So the Committee agreed to ask the County Council for extra relief and to ask the local Education Committee to provide meals and boots for needy children. If it works it looks like some good has been done by the unemployed going to see the Guardians but your dad says they can only do what the Government will allow them to do.

There's been some council elections here. In our ward, Grove Hill, Mrs Levick who is an Independent and was the councillor for six years and was the Mayoress was beaten by Alfred Edwards who was standing for Labour. The Gazette calls the Labour Party candidates socialists and drives Stan

Cole mad. Anyway Mr Edwards is the managing director of a diamond grit merchants whatever that means. The Gazette said he's the only Labour councillor who is an employer and there is talk of him standing for Parliament. Mrs Levick lost by 83 votes and she said she will not stand again which is a shame. Mrs Levinson asked me who I voted for and I didn't fancy saying it's a secret ballot so I told her Mrs Levick which was true. That pleased her and she said what a clever woman Mrs Levick is. She was the chairman of the Hospital Committee. I was in two minds who to vote for because like everybody else round here I am against the means test but at the same time Stan has been on so much about the Labour Party candidates not being socialists I thought well if Mr Edwards isn't a socialist what is the point of voting for him. Your dad asked me who I voted for so I asked him who he voted for and when he said who do you think I voted for I said well who do you think I voted for. So he left it at that but I don't know for certain who he voted for, I can make a guess but if Mr Edwards isn't a socialist I could be wrong. Stan Cole said he didn't vote for any of them, he just wrote on his ballot paper Down with the Means Test, Up the working class, which I suppose relieved his feelings though I don't know what it did for the revolution.

The Americans have got a new President. Mr Franklin Roosevelt beat President Hoover in the election and he takes over in January. Mr Roosevelt is from the Democrat Party and their policy is to end prohibition, reduce tariffs on imports and introduce unemployment insurance.

Two men have written an account of why and how the South Gare was built, the breakwater to you and me. They say many ships were sunk in the Tees Bay and that was the reason for the South Gare. They used five million tons of slag and eighteen thousand tons of cement. When the foundation stone was laid in 1863 the toffs had a banquet for a hundred of them in Redcar. Stan was reading this out to us and you can imagine what he said about that. After hard work like that they'd need a break and so on and on and on. Sadie was in at the time and she tried to get Stan going by talking about the Bank of England's Conversion schemes and asking him whether he was going to cash his Government bonds or convert them into the new ones. Stan didn't know what she was talking about apart from the fact that he knew he has no Government bonds so Sadie explained. Sadie's got a bit of a brain and reading about shares has gone to her head. She seems to have an obsession but at the same time know what she's talking about. Anyway what it's all about. When the Government needs more money than it can raise from taxes it borrows and it does this by issuing bonds which people can buy. The Government says when they will pay the money back and pays them interest until the day they pay back. Well the Government needed money badly during the war and they were paying five per cent interest. Now the pay back day has arrived and people can either have their money back or have a new bond which pays only two per cent interest. It's saving the country millions of pounds because people have to lend their money to somebody and with the state of industry it's risky buying shares so they are buying the Government bonds. It was interesting listening to Sadie because none of us knew about this. Why should we, we don't have money to buy shares or bonds. It's good for me as well because when Mrs Levinson is giving me one of her lectures it's easier for me to follow and she gets a good impression of me. She thinks I am quick on the uptake. I don't think it's any good for the fellas that go in Stan Cole's shed because they just say there's no solution to unemployment as long as we have a capitalist government.

Have you heard about the French submarine that sank in July. With you being in the Navy you might have heard. Anyway in case you haven't the captain has to face a court martial for the loss of the submarine. He must have been on the bridge when it sank because there were only seven survivors out of 69 in the crew. That must have been awful for their families.

Well it's time to go. The jam and bread kid is due anytime now. Everybody asks to be remembered. I was talking to Sylvia in the Stores. She said your letter has arrived and she will be replying. So Tara till my next letter.

Your everloving,
Mam
PS Boro 0 Derby County 3

Friday 18 November 1932

Dear Bob,

Well here I am again with my weekly letter hoping that you are well as leaves all here. Writing this letter to you every week really gives me pleasure. Perhaps I have missed out on something but with my education I can't imagine what.

I've been reading that the Americans have elected a new President, Mr Roosevelt who is from the Democrat Party. He beat President Hoover easily. It says that Mr Hoover won in only six States out of 48. I didn't know there were 48 States so that's something else I've learned and I am passing it on to you in case you get a question in your exams. The Democrats are against prohibition, they want lower tariffs on trade and they want State unemployment insurance. When you think they don't even have the dole it's no wonder that Mr Roosevelt won.

You know the two Pears soap advertisements hanging on our front kitchen wall that I kid Jimmy about. Well he still thinks that the lady with the dark hair is me and the blonde is your auntie Pam. The other day I caught him staring at the picture of the dark haired lady and I asked him what he was doing. So he said Mam, you were really very beautiful weren't you. Well I don't know what they are teaching Jimmy at school but I've noticed that lately he has been having trouble with his tenses. So I'm thinking of holding a slice of jam and bread just out of his reach and saying today we are going to learn tenses, you were, you are, you were, you are. He'll soon get the idea. They say the way to a man's heart is through his stomach though I'm not sure about the way to their brains.

There's been a National Boys and Girls Book week here and there was a pageant in St John's Hall with 250 children there. Prizes were presented to children who had won in competitions and one of the boys was Peter Collingwood who is in the same class at Marton Grove as our Jimmy. His dad is a teacher at Hugh Bell and they live at the bottom of Meadowfield Avenue.

The Germans have had another election, I think that is the fifth in a year. Nobody in Sunnyside can understand it so I asked Mrs Levinson, her husband has been to Germany and so I thought she might know and sure enough she did. She said the Germans have a different way of electing their Parliament to us. Here we vote for an MP in every constituency and there are 615, and the Party that wins the majority of constituencies has a majority of MPs in Parliament so they form the Government. The votes that the parties get who do not win in that constituency do not count for anything.

In Germany instead of having a lot of constituencies with candidates in every constituency like us, the people vote for a political party. Each Party has a list of candidates and the number of MPs they get is the same as the percentage of the votes they get. So if the Nazi Party gets 40 per cent of the votes they get 40 per cent of the seats in Parliament. They have a list of names with the leaders at the top and they work down the list till they have the 40 per cent. Mrs Levinson said that this results in no party having a majority in Parliament because all the small parties get MPs. So they can only get a government if some parties combine to form a majority and the main parties, the Nazis, the Communists and the Socialists will not join to form a Government. I remember what Stan Cole told me that the Labour Party formed a Government in 1924 and in 1929 and they didn't have a majority in Parliament. Mrs Levinson said that was because the other parties let them but as soon as Labour did something that they disagreed with they voted them out.

So because no Party has a majority Germany is governed by a Chancellor who is appointed by the President, but he has just resigned. The Chancellor I mean. The Nazis want the President to appoint Hitler to be Chancellor but he doesn't want to. Anyway he is meeting Hitler tomorrow.

Eston Council have voted to set up soup kitchens for children in South Bank because they are going to school without any breakfast. It's no wonder when you think that a family with three people in it gets 23 shillings a week and pay eleven shillings rent. Bring out my soap box, I feel a speech coming on. Anyway there's one thing for sure our Jimmy's not going to school without something to eat inside him. There's a row going on in the letters in the Gazette about landlords. In East Street, that's over the railway near the transporter houses are divided up into single rooms and whole families are living in one room and they are being charged six shillings and eight shillings a week. We are really lucky having a council house with a bathroom and a garden at the front and the back.

Newhouses Sports Club have held a crazy night, and it must have been crazy because they had a yo yo competition. Imagine adults playing with yo yos. Then they had a demonstration by a fifteen year old boy called Kenneth Mayley who is the yo yo champion of London. He's here giving demonstrations round Teesside.

I was round at Sylvia's mother's house. Sylvia is getting on marvelous with the piano and she can read music now.

Sadie came over and she was livid. Thousands of ex-service men took part in Armistice Day in Dublin and when it was ended gangs of republicans attacked people to take their poppies. The police had to use their batons and there are forty people in hospital. That's because republicans are opposed to Armistice Day. In the Irish Parliament they didn't observe the two minutes silence and only a few of them wore poppies. Sadie is really angry because all those Irishmen who fought against the Germans should be honoured. After all lots of them lost their lives. We went to the cenotaph and Paddy and Sadie came with us. Would you believe it but during the two minutes silence a works buzzer blew. There were lots there. The Mayor laid a wreath and buglers from the Green Howards sounded the Last Post. There was a service led by the Vicar of All Saints Church and we all sang 'O God Our Help in Ages Past' with the Salvation Army band. I don't know what to make of this but In Newcastle three communists started shouting during the two minutes silence and the police had to rescue them from an angry mob and in Middlesbrough the fascist blackshirts were at the cenotaph as good as gold.

I don't know whether Mrs Nelson has got this Advert in her scrap book but I'll show her it. "Why married women lose their looks. Even if you have all the cares of a household on your shoulders you needn't lose your looks. If you find yourself giving way to worry, find your looks going, your nerves getting jumpy, take a glass of Wincarnis at 11.30, another in the afternoon and one before you go to bed." I don't know who thinks these adverts up but they must think we are made of money as well as being silly. What would help to end my worries would be your dad getting a job, not me drinking three glasses of wine a day on the dole, and anyway I haven't lost my looks. Sez me. Well, it's time please again, school is out and trouble is on his way, so till next time look after yourself. Everybody asks to be remembered.

Tara for now,
Your everloving,
Mam.
PS Boro 1 Blackpool 3

Friday 25 November 1932

Dear Bob,

How are you enjoying the sun in Bermuda? We could do with some here, it has been cold and drizzling. But Christmas is coming and I can't imagine Christmas in a hot climate. It wouldn't seem like Christmas without snow or frost. We hear that there's been a terrible hurricane in the Caribbean with hundreds of people killed and their sugar and banana crops destroyed. Are you anywhere near that? It must be awful for the people there.

Your dad and me went to the cemetery to visit our Mary's grave. I pray to God for Mary and your dad curses the Government. I get comfort from prayer and your dad just gets worked up. I feel so sorry for him. I always hoped he would improve with time but he seems to be getting worse. He hasn't a good word to say for the Government and he brings our Mary into it. He says they should spend more money finding out what causes these illnesses and how to cure them. He is so frustrated. I was taught at Sunday school that hating people doesn't do any good. The person who is hated doesn't feel anything but the person who is doing the hating is getting all worked up inside and that damages them. Having said that Dracula has just rode past and I hate him. But so does everybody else so perhaps I'll get away with it.

What do you think of this? An American professor has said that Britain's difficulties are caused by the flapper vote, by which he means women's votes. If an educated man thinks that women are flappers, and I suppose that must include his own mother, what are uneducated men to think. He said that women run to extremes and it is women's fault that America has prohibition. How does he make that out. This is a professor talking. He said if women stayed at home instead of taking up politics there would be less crime, and he said that in twenty years time there will be more women than men and then women will rule the country and what a disaster that will be. Well who does he think is ruling the country now and look how much unemployment there is and who did the flappers vote for if it wasn't men.

Mrs Nelson has a very funny advert in her scrap book. It's a strip cartoon and it shows two city gents walking down a street when a thug appears and knocks the biggest one out. The smaller city gent then knocks him out and he doesn't even lose his bowler hat. Then he pulls a bottle of Enos Fruit Salt out of his pocket and holds it up in front of his pal who is slumped against the wall. If that is what Enos Fruit Salt will do for you I thought you should know in case anybody picks on you you know what to do. Just carry a bottle in your pocket. I won't recommend it to your dad, I can't afford it and anyway any criminal that thought of having a go at your dad needs the bottle of Enos fruit salts. He'd also need his head looking at.

Sadie came over, Mr Muir had been pulling her and Paddy's legs about an article he'd read, What is an Irishman. Scientists to answer the Question. Stan Cole said it's a man who has been oppressed by the English for centuries. So Mr Muir said well how about the Scots. It only needed Taffy Evans to come along to make a trio. Just think, your dad and me are English and we have been oppressing that lot for centuries. Stan can really put the cat among the pigeons. When Ta Ta Pet came in we asked him what he thought, he goes to night school. So he said who are the English which had us puzzled for a bit because we thought that was us then he went on about the invaders who settled here, the Vikings, the Romans, the Normans, the Angles and the Saxons. Go to Geordieland, you don't know what they're talking about half the time he said. Anyway Harvard University in America is carrying out a survey lasting five years. They are excavating for evidence of Irish life in prehistoric and early Christian times. Come to think about it if a man with a name like de Valera is an Irishman I'm a Chinaman, well woman.

Durham County Council has refused to carry out the means test so the Government has moved in and they are going to do it. Middlesbrough council was told that is what would happen here if they refused so they said it would be better to have local people who know the area doing it because they would be more understanding than civil servants from London. So they do it and they've just announced how much money they've saved for the Government. They've reduced transitional payment for nearly 5,000 people and refused it altogether for another 1,800 and saved the government £2,500 a week. Dracula will have had a hand in that. There's a very bitter letter in the Gazette by a man who says that this has reduced the amount of money people can spend in Middlesbrough and it's no wonder that shops are closing. He didn't say if he has a shop.

Talking about money President Hoover is saying that Britain must pay the interest on its debts to America by December 15 and that is £28million. He is opposed to canceling the debt. Mrs Levinson was livid about it because she said it was not really our debt, we had paid but we had also promised to pay the debt of our allies in the war and they would pay us but they haven't. They are saying that Mr Roosevelt will not demand payment but he doesn't take over until January. He is in favour of negotiating with the countries that owe them money about ending tariffs and reducing spending on armaments. I asked Mrs Levinson what she thought about that because she is in favour of tariffs and wants us to spend more on armaments because of Germany. So she said that if all countries will end tariffs and cut spending on arms she would agree with Mr Roosevelt.

It's all very complicated. Local bazaars are my level. Sadie helped out at the St Joseph's sale of work to raise money for a new church which Father Mullen hopes to start building early next year. I helped out at All Saints church four days bazaar and I persuaded your dad too as well The Reverend Hill said they raised £800 and they had door to door collections in the parish during they year. They use the money to help the poor of the parish but he is in hot water with some of the councillors. He said that parts of the parish are slums and the councillors got their bowels in an uproar about it. But his Assistant priest wrote a letter to the Gazette and he said that the Reverend Hill had been misunderstood. He didn't say it was all a slum, but there are houses that are let out in single rooms in which families live and have to do everything.

Mrs Levinson was worried about what is happening in Germany. The Chancellor Herr von Papen has resigned because he has hardly any supporters in the Reichstag, that's their Parliament. So President von Hindenburg has asked Herr Hitler if he would be Chancellor but on the condition that he can get a majority in the Reichstag. Hitler has gone away to think about it. He wants to be Chancellor but how can he get a majority in the Reichstag. Mrs Levinson is worried that somebody will do a deal with him, and she says that if they do Hitler will take Germany to war. Stan Cole says that if Hitler becomes Chancellor he will make such a mess of things that the people will throw him out. So there are two different stories but which one is right. The Nazis are doing such terrible things in Germany, beating people up and killing people that I hope Hitler can't get a majority. It isn't like in England.

I've received your card saying that you might be home for the New Year because you might be leaving HMS Norfolk. That is good news and we will be looking forward to you coming home. You didn't say why you might be leaving HMS Norfolk and might doesn't mean definite. So I suppose you will explain when it becomes definite.

I'll have to go now. The jam and bread kid's been in but I am running late and your dad will be in for his tea soon so Tara for now. Everybody asks to be remembered,

Your everloving,
Mam
PS Boro 0 Everton 2

Friday 2 December 1932

Dear Bob,

How are you keeping? No need to answer it's just my usual question but I like to know. We are hoping that you will be home for the New Year though we still don't know why you might be leaving HMS Norfolk. We are all looking forward to seeing you and I know that Sylvia is but she is as much in the dark as the rest of us. She was round last Saturday night and I did her hair for her. I have become her regular hairdresser now.

There's been a dreadful accident here in the Navy. Have you heard about it. One of our submarines, HMS Thames, was coming home to Portsmouth in heavy seas and two men, a seaman and a signalman were swept overboard. It is so awful just thinking of them and then their families expecting them home not dreaming anything like this could happen in peacetime. I am trying not to think about it but it keeps coming into my mind. Life goes on they say, and it does for us, but for them it's changed forever.

Sadie was in. She got a letter from her sister Pat in Canada and another one from Kathleen in London. Kathleen is coming for Christmas though there's no chance of Pat making it. Anyway I told you that the last time Pat wrote she was in Halifax in Nova Scotia. Well now she's moved. She had a job in a bank in Halifax but it was only temporary, then they offered her a regular job but in Toronto so she took it. So that's where she is now. She's a book keeper or an accountant, something like that I don't know the difference. She's been very lucky getting a job, she's told Sadie what it is like in Canada for work and it is worse than here. Unemployment is 18% that's nearly one in five out of work and there is no unemployment insurance, it's every man for himself. That's what Pat said, not me. In Toronto there has been a violent demonstration of the unemployed like everywhere else in Canada and the Government has been using the Mounties to prevent riots. I remember reading that the Canadian Government was telling people who had migrated there to go home and if they didn't they were arrested and sent back in handcuffs.

It's bad here but at least we have the insurance scheme which gives us the dole for a while then transitional benefit before we have to go on the pancrack. I don't want to be dependent on Dracula saying what we are entitled to. That man would shop his own mother. He's just rode past like god almighty on his sit up and beg. Gyp can't be out, at least I can't hear him. Your dad was out last night with Sam Maynard catching rabbits. It's a big help but my heart is in my mouth all the time they are out and I can hardly get to sleep for worrying. So far we've been lucky. I don't know why but perhaps its because Sam always gives a rabbit to Mrs Masterman so maybe that helps. The police have had a wages cut so I don't suppose Mr Masterman is going to go out of his way to catch poachers, especially those he knows and boozes with in the Cleveland. Your dad was saying that he is a good singer, he has a good base voice.

Lieutenant Commander Bower who is the Conservative MP for Cleveland said in the House of Commons that at the battle of Jutland he saw a battleship blow up with a thousand men on board. He said many Navy officers do not think that we will be able to use battleships in the Far East and the Far West because they need bases. He thinks if we are going to have battleships the German pocket battleship will be best. He said we are not spending too much on the Navy but we are spending it on the wrong things. What do you think? Anyway he said another arms race will end in war and the Navy should be part of an international police force keeping the peace.

The French have launched a new submarine, they say it can travel at 20 knots on the surface and ten knots submerged. Is that good? Notice that I said knots and not knots an hour, you see your old mam is learning.

Mrs Levinson had the ginger biscuits out when I was round there. First of all she asked me if I would bake a Christmas cake for her and when I said I would she sent me round to the shops to buy the ingredients and she told me to get enough for one for us as well. I thought that was good of her but when you think about it I still had to do the cleaning so it is really extra time. But I don't mind, it's no trouble and I'll make it here in our oven and she gave me sixpence to pay for the gas.

Anyway when I got back from the shops she had the biscuits out and started to tell me about a Russian man called Zinoviev. She said that he was a leading communist in Russia and was the chairman of the Communist International. Anyway he sent a letter to the Communist Party in Britain in

1924 telling them that the Communist International wanted more revolutionary propaganda in the British army and navy. Then the Daily Mail got hold of a copy of this letter and they published it and it lost the General Election for the Labour Party. Mrs Levinson said she was telling me this out of interest because Mr Zinoviev had just died and he was only 49. She said he didn't die, just like that, he was expelled from the Communist Party for counter revolutionary activity, whatever that is, and then he died. She says he was shot and that's what happens when communists get power. She wasn't really telling me this out of interest, at least I don't think so. She knows that I know Stan Cole and she knows about Stan Cole's politics, everybody knows about Stan Cole's politics, you couldn't live in Grove Hill or anywhere near and not know about Stan Cole's politics. I think Mrs Levinson thought I would tell Stan what she said and she was right. Maybe she wants to stop Stan from influencing me. Anyway I did tell Stan and he said the letter was a forgery and it had done its job. So that was Stan's reply to that.

Mrs Levinson's sister is coming for two weeks. That's the one who lives in London and used to throw bricks through shop windows to get votes for women and paid me last Christmas for helping her with the Dance of the Seven Dusters. I'm looking forward to her coming, she's a bit of a laugh and I think she might have a screw loose, well that seems an unkind thing to say, she is very kind hearted so maybe just half a screw a bit loose but she's all for the working class. It sounds so funny to hear her going on about the working class in her posh accent. You just don't expect it. She is very good on the piano and it is a treat to be doing the cleaning and listening to her at the same time.

Your dad and me went to see the new wing of the North Ormesby hospital. They allowed the public to go round. It's very modern and they are calling it the Sister Elizabeth wing after the Mother Superior of the Holy Rood who used to be the matron. I used to be a ward maid there doing the cleaning.

That's all for this time. School is out and the jam and bread kid hasn't arrived yet but he can't be far away, so I better be ready with the bread knife. Did I tell you that your dad said he needed some new socks so Jimmy said why don't you smoke Clubs cigarettes you get a pair free if you smoke them and you only have to send 60 empty packets. Jimmy's arithmetic isn't what it should be. Five cigs for twopence, multiply by 60 and

you have a ten shillings pair of socks. I must go, I hear him now.
Tara for now. Everybody asks to be remembered.
Your everloving,
Mam.
PS Arsenal 4 Boro 2

Friday 9 December 1932

Dear Bob,

Your letter has arrived telling us that you will be home soon. We hope it is going to be for Christmas or the New Year so it's fingers crossed, but why are you leaving the Norfolk. Does this mean that you are coming home to join another ship? We are full of questions here so tell us in your next letter.

The Navy is having another go at raising the submarine M2. The last time they tried they nearly succeeded then a hawser snapped. They are hoping to get her up this time and then they are going to tow her into dry dock in Portsmouth. It will be an awful job for the men who have to get all the bodies out and I feel so sorry for the families of the crew who died. I wonder if they will all be buried in Portsmouth or whether they will be sent home to be buried.

Isn't it strange how things that you think are good turn out to have a bad side, like heads and tails on coins, there seems to be two sides to everything. In the Settlement on Newport Road they are teaching unemployed men how to do things, and one of them is how to mend boots. You would think that was a good thing, I did, then a man from Haverton Hill writes a letter in the Gazette saying that he is unemployed but he served his time learning to be a boot repairer and he says that if these charitable men and women in the Settlement teach the unemployed to mend boots he and many others who served their time will be ruined. He says the men who will be taught in the Settlement will not be skilled enough to do a good job though they will be able to mend their own boots. So there you are, a good turn for one turns out to be a bad turn for others.

Another man from Redcar has written in saying that the tap water in Redcar smells and tastes awful and he wants to know why. He's put the cat among the pigeons with that and there are replies saying it not like that in some parts of Redcar and somebody else wants to know if it is chlorine in the water.

Dorman Long made a film of the building of Sydney Bridge and they are going to show it at the Hippodrome for three mornings in January so that school children can see it in the Christmas holidays. I wouldn't mind seeing it myself.

Greta Garbo is on at the Gaumont in 'As You Desire Me'. I fancied seeing that and I thought that your dad might have liked to go to see the second picture, Mickey Mouse in 'Mad Dog' but your dad said it might be too emotional for him and anyway we haven't any money which is when I got emotional because I know that on Saturday night he will have the money to go in the Cleveland. You would think he saw enough of Stan Cole and the others who go in Stan's shed but I suppose they see the Cleveland as a bit of relaxation after tiring their brains out solving the country's problems in Stan's shed.

There's an article in the Gazette saying that Middlesbrough has spent one and a half million pounds since 1921 on building houses. They built 1,755 houses in Grove Hill. I would never have thought they had built that many in Grove Hill. Some of them were built by Dorman Long with steel frames and out of concrete. They will be the houses in Deepdale and Fairfield I suppose. I wouldn't fancy living in one of them and anyway Deepdale always floods so I am glad we got Sunnyside.

Well Hitler wasn't appointed Chancellor in Germany after all. The President said he could be Chancellor if he could get a majority in the Reichstag, that's the German Parliament and he couldn't so President von Hindenburg has appointed a soldier General Von Schleicher. He hasn't got a majority either but the socialists have said they want to see what his programme is before they decide whether to support him or not. The Nazis and the Communists are definitely opposed so I wonder how it will work out. I wonder if they will have another election, that would make six in a year.

There's still a big argument about Britain paying its war debt to America. They are saying in the paper that there was an agreement at Lausanne which is in Switzerland that Germany wouldn't have to pay any more reparations. Now France is saying that if Germany doesn't pay them they are not going to pay America which leaves us because our Government has said it will pay but we can't go on paying without getting the money owed to us. It might change after Mr Roosevelt takes over but that is not till next January and we have to pay in December. Mr Levinson was saying that trying to force the Germans to pay will damage the world economy and he's a businessman so he should know what he's talking about. He's also an expert on Germany because he goes there on business. I think I told you that he was in military intelligence during the war. I told Stan Cole that once when Stan was in here laying the law down about Germany and Stan said there is no such thing as military intelligence because how could any intelligent General order men to march towards machine guns to be slaughtered.

Have you heard that the Persian government is wanting to end the oil concession that they agreed with the Anglo-Persian Oil Company. The agreement was that the oil company had permission to get the oil out for sixty years in return for the Persian Government getting sixteen per cent of the profits. Things have been alright as long as there were big profits but the profits have gone down and so the Persian Government is talking about ending the concession and our Government is saying they have no right to do that and if they do the Government will do whatever it has to do to protect British lives and property. So it looks like more trouble unless they can get an agreement. It's the Persians' oil so they do have a point. They are saying they need the money for their people which I think is right but as usual I can see both sides and it was British investment and experts who have got the oil out. Do you think I would make a good politician. Stan Cole says that seeing all sides means you never do anything and I suppose he is right, I would be a right old ditherer.

Well, just one bit of news that will surprise you, it certainly surprised me. The Palladium had a staff dance in the Assembly Rooms and there were 180 people there. There can't be more than twenty on the staff. I've been trying to do a count but have given up but that must be the limit. Anyway I thought you would like to know that. It won't be long before you are going to the Palladium yourself.

That's all for this time. I had to stop to give you know who a slice of jam and bread and peace was restored. Everybody asks to be remembered so tara for now,

Your everloving,

Mam

PS Boro 3 West Bromwich Albion 1. Blackmore scored a hat trick. I wonder why they call scoring three goals a hat trick. It's not as if he wearing a hat.

Friday 16 December 1932

Dear Bob,

Your letter has arrived telling us that you have volunteered for submarines and that you will be home early in January to go to HMS Dolphin for training. Well it's your life and I can't tell you what to do and you will know why you have volunteered for submarines but it really does worry me. They seem to be so dangerous and we read of submarines sinking so I can only hope that you have made a wise decision and that you are going to be safe. Perhaps they will improve in peacetime and we have to hope there isn't another war.

Ta Ta Pet was in as per usual on his round. He'd been in Mrs Turnbull's first and they'd been at her rhubarb wine and he was in a right state so we had to put his bike in our back arch just like last year. He's going to some insurance agents do at Christmas and he is going to recite The Charge of the Light Brigade and being the state he was in he thought our house for some reason would be a good place to rehearse but he couldn't remember the second verse so he asked your dad. He thought that because your dad was in the army that he would know The Charge of the Light Brigade. Sometimes I wonder about Ta Ta Pet. Your dad said he didn't know The Charge of the Light Brigade, he was in the infantry not the cavalry and they had to charge the German trenches on foot. Fancy asking your dad that, he doesn't know the first line of Daffodils never mind the second verse of anything.

Your dad went to a meeting to hear George Hardie who is Kier Hardie's brother. I said who is Kier Hardie when he's all there and your dad said he was the man who started the Labour Party so he probably had something to say that was worth the walk down the town. Anyway he told me that Mr Hardie said that tariffs on trade were only to protect inefficiency in industry and did not help British industry. He said that the iron and steel bosses asked the Government to introduce the tariffs to protect our iron and steel industry and to convince the Government they imported large amounts of iron and steel. This convinced Members of Parliament to introduce the tariffs but the real reason was to protect their own inefficiency. That was really crafty if it was true. He said British industry was built up on free trade and we should go back to it. I asked Mrs Levinson what she thought about that because she is in favour of tariffs and she isn't an iron and steel boss and she said Mr Hardie was living in the past. Britain was the first industrialised nation in the world and free trade suited us then because there was no competition but that is no longer the case. Is it any wonder that I'm confused. I wish I hadn't asked her then I would have been happy with the truth according to George Hardie. Then I read in the Gazette that the Cleveland Institute of Engineers says Teesside blast furnaces are too small and are obsolete. The Germans have found a way to save energy called Warmestelle which reduces the amount of coal they have to use. So there must be something in what Mr Hardie says.

I was stood chatting at the gate with Mrs Maynard, Sadie and Mrs Turner and Mrs Wilson when Dracula came riding down the street. Gyp was out and sraightaway he was after Dracula barking and snapping at him. We were all laughing then Mrs Wilson said what a world this is when we have to have a dog to speak up for us. We were supposed to laugh but that really depressed me and when I came in I felt so down that I got down on my knees with a duster and took it out on the lino. That relieved my feelings and I am alright again. Sadie came in and we had a cup of tea and talked about it and Sadie was saying well what else can we do and the answer is keep smiling. Don't let them get you down.

The Volcanic Amateur Film Society have made a film of Middlesbrough to include in their Round Teesside. They've already made a film of the Redcar councillors opening an aged people's home. Anyway In Middlesbrough they filmed a grand march past the Town Hall and round Victoria Gardens led by the mace bearer, then two policemen carrying the coat of arms then the Mayor dressed in his red robes then the Aldermen in their fur trimmed gowns and then the councillors in their blue gowns then the officers. You should have heard what Stan Cole had to say about that. He said Dracula should have been in front on his bike. But they did make a film of other parts of the Boro like the Boro football team in action and Jack Hatfield at the baths.

A thing that interests me especially in Middlesbrough is the market down the town. Sadie and me go down there every Saturday night and wait for the prices to drop. Anyway the stall holders are wanting a new covered market on Newport Road and at their annual dinner and dance in the Town Hall they had the Mayor there to talk about it. He said the council was in favour of a new market but that will mean buying some expensive property to demolish and they will have to wait for more prosperous times. The oldest stall holder who used to sell fruit and vegetables died recently and the oldest one now is called Mrs Robertson, she is 84 and she was born in the market place and baptised in St Hilda's church. That's a lovely old church and reading all this is like seeing Middlesbrough's history passing before our eyes like on a cinematograph.

Well Bob, a final thought. You know I told you that we have to pay millions of pounds to America off our debt from the war. Well George Bernard Shaw who is a famous Irishman and writes plays was setting off on a world tour at Victoria railway station and he said Ireland should be handed over to America in lieu of our debt. Sadie was not pleased about that and she said Ireland should be given back to the Irish but first they should get rid of Mr De Valera. That's all for another week so look after yourself and we hope to see you soon. Jimmy asks to be remembered round a slice of jam and bread. So does everybody else. So tara for now.

Your ever loving,

Mam

PS Boro 1 Sheffield Wednesday 2. I have to tell you that it would have been different but the Boro had two men injured and so were playing with nine men.

Friday 23 December 1932

Dear Bob,

I have just received your letter saying that you will definitely be coming home but that it will be early in the New Year and you will explain everything then. Harry Robson was home on leave and he came to see us and to ask about you. I asked him what sort of ship HMS Dolphin is and he said it is a training school at Portsmouth for men going on submarines. So he was only telling us something we already knew but somehow it's more believable being told face to face than in a letter.

Sadie's sister Kathleen has come for Christmas. I think she's here for ten days. I told you she's a teacher and about her coming here in the summer holidays. Well she came in with Sadie at the same time as Ta Ta Pet. I know why Sadie came in then, to talk to Ta Ta Pet about shares. Any way Jimmy was going to go out carol singing but just before he went out he asked me where Orry and Tar is. I said Orry and Tar. Orry and Tar. I hadn't heard of them but I thought they might be Scottish islands so I told him to ask his dad who was sitting in the corner with his nose in his dictionary. Your dad has worked in Scotland in the shipyards so I thought he might know but he said he didn't work on any Scottish islands and he'd never heard of any called Orry and Tar. Sadie said don't ask me I don't know anything about geography and Kathleen and Ta Ta Pet didn't know. So I asked Jimmy why he wanted to know and he said it was in a carol. So I said what carol and I told him to sing it so he started. We three Kings of Orry and Tar, Bearing gifts we travel afar. Well, I put my hands over my face to stop myself laughing. Out of the corner of my eye I could see your dad. He'd put his dictionary over his face but I could see his body shaking. Sadie and Kathleen went over to the window pretending to look out to see if it was snowing. Ta Ta Pet just sat there. He's good like that. So I did my best to keep my face straight and explained to him that it is We three Kings of Orient are. He did this once before. Did I tell you about it. It was a song at school God Bless the Prince of Wales and Jimmy asked me why they wanted God to let the prairie echo and I had to explain to him that it is not let the prairie echo, it is let the prayer re-echo. He's got a great imagination our Jimmy, I think he'll grow up to be a politician.

Any way to get back to what I was talking about. Kathleen said to Jimmy if you are going out carol singing how about starting here and I will give you a threepenny bit, which was very good of her. Well they say you should never look a gift horse in the mouth and Jimmy wasn't going to. So he said he would sing While Shepherds Watched. So Kathleen said right well you start and we'll all join in. Little did she know there's While Shepherds Watched and there's While Shepherds Watched as the kids round here sing it. As he thought this was a special occasion Jimmy sang the second version.

While Shepherds watched their tungy tops
All boiling in a pot
The Angel of the Lord came down
And pinched the blinking lot.

We were all in stitches and as soon as we stopped laughing one of us would start up again.

Kathleen is a teacher and she can organise things so she said how about getting together to sing some carols in the street. Sylvia came round and she brought a lantern and there was seven of us sang carols in the middle of Sunnyside. Good King Wenceslas, O Come all ye Faithful, Away in a Manger, Silent Night, God Bless ye Merry Gentlemen, While Shepherds Watched, We three kings of Orry and Tar, Kathleen had a job keeping her face straight when we came to that one, and more. We had a really good sing song. Then we went into

Sadie's. Kathleen had made a bowl of punch to warm us up. I've never drunk punch before, I don't even know what it is but it tasted good and after standing out there in the cold it was really good. Before we drank it Kathleen raised her glass and said a toast, Women of the world unite, You have nothing to lose but your inferiority complexes. I think she must have heard Stan Cole's motto, Workers of the world unite, you have nothing to lose but your chains. Women are not allowed to be teachers if they are married so if any woman teacher wants to get married she has to resign or get the sack and Kath does not agree with that. If Kathleen lived here I wouldn't be surprised if there would be a Kathleen's shed like Stan Cole's.

Well it's payday for America. Britain has paid them nearly twenty million pounds in gold. France and some others are refusing to pay. The French Government wanted to pay but their Parliament wouldn't let them so the Government has resigned. Mrs Levinson said her husband told her it won't affect Britain very much because it is only a small part of our gold reserves but that doesn't make it right. Why should we be paying while others are refusing and getting away with it. You know I told you about the Persian Government going to end their agreement letting the British oil company get the oil out of the ground. Well the Government has referred it to the League of Nations to try to get an agreement there. That's better than going to war which is what it looked like when our Government said they would do what was necessary to protect British lives and property.

How about this? Dorman Long lost over two hundred and forty thousand pounds on the Sydney bridge contract. Your dad said this was because the value of the Australian pound fell to sixteen shillings in British currency and Dorman Long were paid in Australian pounds. Also Dorman Long were going to sell a lot of the equipment they used to Australian companies but they couldn't afford to buy it so Dorman Long had to bring it home. It just seems as if everything is going wrong for us and to rub salt in the wound the Boro lost to Leeds.

Well, I'll just get the jam and bread out. Mam I'm starving has just arrived. He said he thinks he can hold out till I finish this letter. So tara for now. Everybody wishes you a Merry Christmas and a Happy New Year. There's no point in my writing again because you will be home before the letter arrives in Bermuda. See you soon.

Your everloving,
Mam
PS Leeds 1 Boro 0.
Stop Press. Urgent. Read this immediately. Your dad has just come in from Stan Cole's shed and he's saying that I have to tell you that William McCrum has died in County Antrim in Northern Ireland. The reason for this urgent piece of important news, and that your dad has just come back from solving the country's problems, is that Mr McCrum is the man who invented the penalty spot in football. It used to be that full backs would handle the ball if it looked like it might be going in the goal or they would trip the other player up if he looked like scoring. It sounds something like politicians. Anyway the other side would be given a free kick but they were not allowed to score from a free kick. So to stop them deliberately handling the ball or tripping the other player up he recommended to the Irish football association that they have the penalty rule that football has today. The British football association adopted the rule in 1891. I hope this helps you pass your exams for promotion and stops you from having sleepless nights.

Friday 30 December 1932

Dear Bob,

Here I am again after all. I said my last letter would be the last to you on the Norfolk but Friday has come and without a letter to write I feel empty. Also I didn't wish you a Happy New Year and that might bring bad luck so here I am wishing you a Happy New Year. I know you won't receive this until you get back to England but I feel all the better for writing it. I expect it will be short but at least your dad will get his PS with the football score.

There's been an awful collision between two ships off Seaham harbour. It was dense fog and a Norwegian ship hit the Gateshead in the middle of her port side and she sank in two minutes and eight of the crew including the captain went down with her. Your dad said it sounds like the Gateshead was traveling down the coast towards the Tees and the Norwegian ship was coming into the Tyne but he thinks there had to be negligence because they both should have been sounding their fog horns. Anyway that's not much comfort to the families and at this time of year. I wonder what sort of Christmas they will have.

There was lots of celebrations here in the hospitals with the wards decorated and the nurses going round the wards singing carols. In the North Riding Infirmary two surgeons dressed up as Father Christmas and went round the children's wards and put a full stocking on every child's bed. That brings tears to me eyes just thinking about it. St Paul's choir went round the wards singing carols and St Johns church choir went round North Ormesby hospital. All the hospitals did something for the children and the other patients. I like Christmas for this sort of thing, it seems to bring the best out in people. The Mayor went to the annual Christmas tea party at the Junior Instruction Centre in Bridge Street and made a speech telling the boys that they had to learn to use their hands and their brains. Then Father Christmas presented him with a mouth organ. Stan Cole had something to say about that and it wasn't complimentary. In Holgate the people in there, and there were 460 of them, I never knew there was that many people in the workhouse, had a special Christmas dinner and the men got tobacco and cigarettes and the women got sweets and fruit. Four thousand children were let into picture houses for nothing and were given presents as well. The Hippodrome was the biggest, but as well the Gaumont, the Pav on Newport Road and even the Palladium. There were seven hundred children at the Palladium but our Jimmy didn't get a ticket. They said it was for the poorest families so that must mean that we are not poor enough. There's an angry letter in the Gazette from a man who signs himself ex-Service man. He said the treat at the Hippodrome was supposed to be for needy children and his children weren't invited even though he is out of work and he knows some men who are working and their children went. I suppose we could get angry but then I think of those folks who are worse off than us. There's been a house fire in Birmingham on Christmas Eve and six children were burned to death. The mother jumped out of a bedroom window with a baby in her arms and she is in hospital with injuries and burns. Her husband has burns. They lived in a house with one room downstairs and one room upstairs with four beds in the one room. We have a front kitchen, a back kitchen, two bedrooms and a bathroom and a garden at the front and the back. I'm not going to complain about our Jimmy not getting in the Palladium. It wouldn't be right.

I told you Mrs Levinson's sister was coming from London. She asked me if Jimmy would like a selection box for Christmas and I said can a duck swim. I told you I thought she had half a screw a little bit loose but I think I was wrong. She's very kind hearted and intelligent. Well that's my opinion no matter what anybody else says.

Your dad just asked me if I was writing about what went on at Christmas so when I said yes he said don't forget to mention the pubs had a one hour extension to 11o'clock. Now that is something I could have forgot without even trying.

Well Bob this was going to be short, there's lots more to write about but I just wanted to say Happy New Year. Everybody sends you their good wishes for the New Year and that includes Sadie's sister Kathleen.

Tara for now. See you soon in the New Year.

Your everloving,

Mam

PS On Christmas Eve the Boro lost to Blackburn Rovers. Blackburn Rovers 4 Boro 2. On the Monday they should have played Sheffield United at Sheffield but the match was cancelled because of fog. They played at Ayresome Park on Tuesday and drew 2 each.

Also available from MUDFOG PRESS, the community publisher for the Tees Valley:

Words On A Map - Poems by Geoff Strange £3.50
ISBN 1-899503-66-8

The Wrong California - Middlesbrough Laureate Poems 2004 by Andy Willoughby £3.50 *ISBN 1-899503-65-X*

A19 - Poems by Geoff Tomlinson £3.50
ISBN 1-899503-64-1

Smoke! A pageant written for Middlesbrough's 150th. birthday by Andy Croft £3.50.
ISBN 1-899503-62-5

Orders

by mail to Mudfog Press, c/o Arts Development, The Stables, Stewart Park,The Grove, Marton, Middlesbrough TS7 8AR
or on line from INP at www.northernpublishers.co.uk